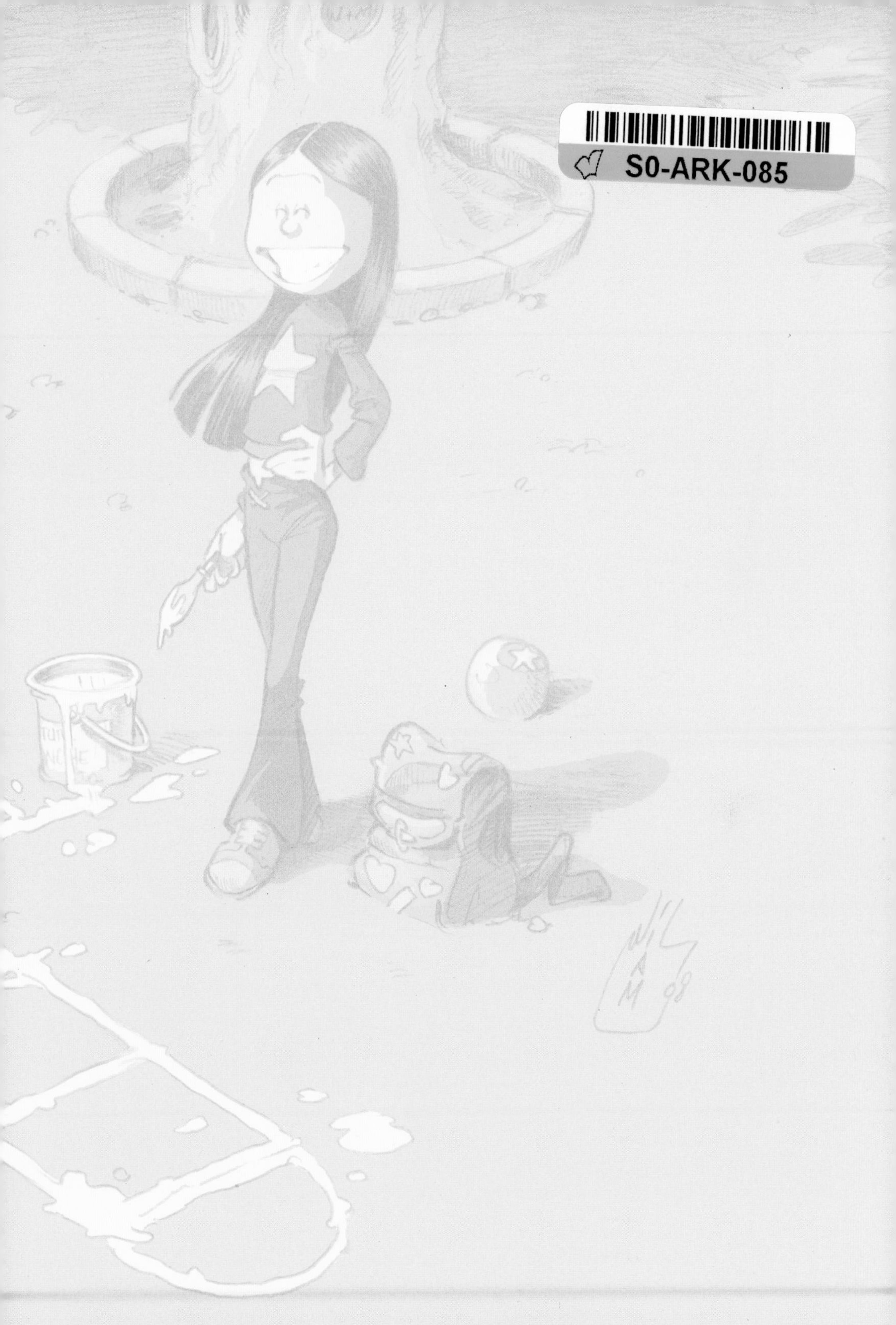

The Sisters

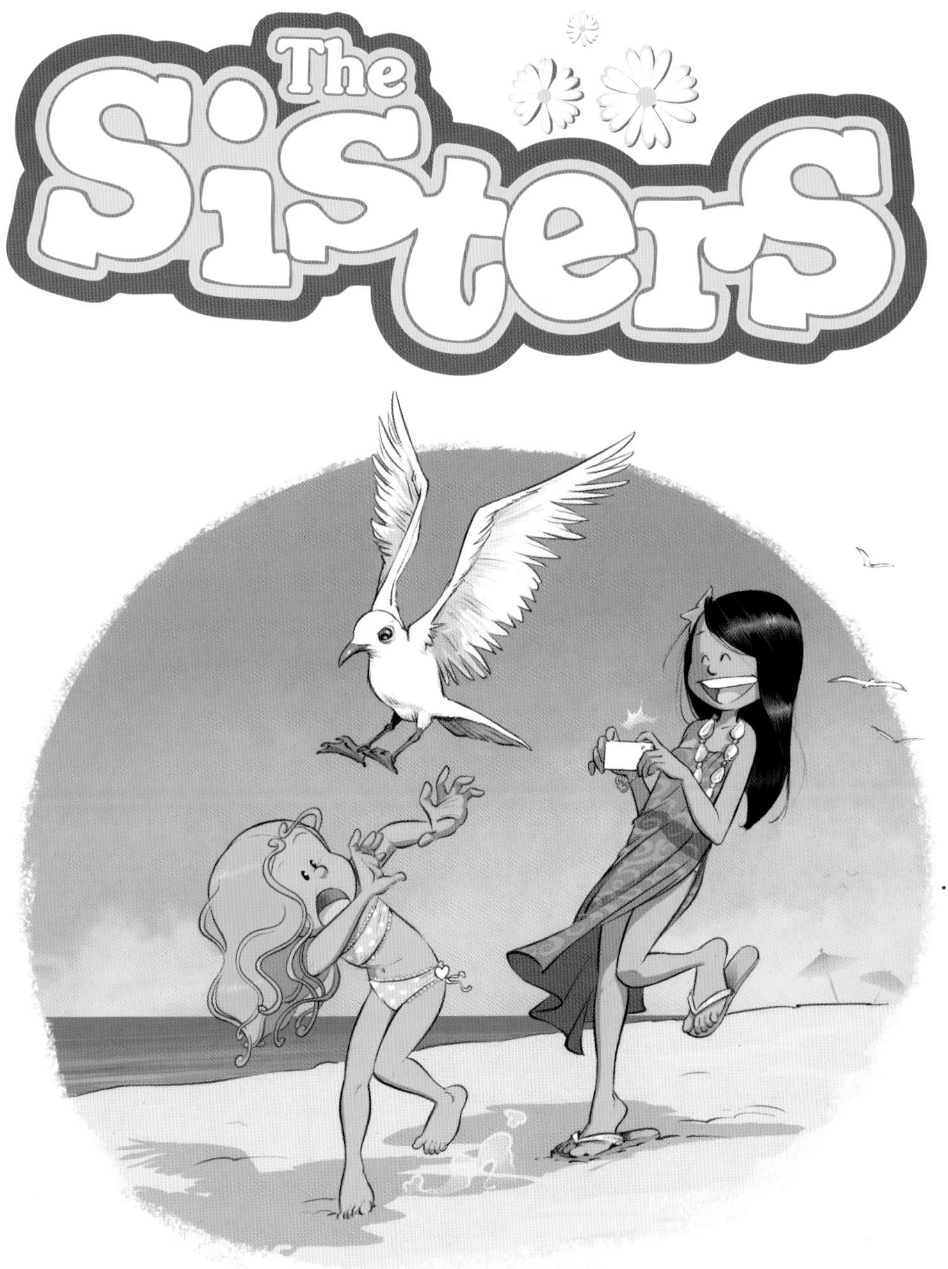

PAPERCUTZ

MORE GREAT GRAPHIC NOVEL SERIES AVAILABLE FROM PAPERCUTZ

THE WILD SMURF

THE SMURFS #21

GARFIELD Show
APPRENTICE SORCERER

THE GARFIELD SHOW #6

Barbie
Fashion Superstar

BARBIE #1

Barbie
PUPPY PARTY

BARBIE PUPPY PARTY

Trolls
Hugs & Friends

TROLLS #1

All-new, full-color Graphic Novel
Geronimo Stilton
THE MYSTERY OF THE PIRATE SHIP

GERONIMO STILTON #17

Thea Stilton
MYSTERY AT SEA

THEA STILTON #6

Nancy Drew DIARIES
CAROLYN KEENE

NANCY DREW DIARIES #7

The Lunch Witch

THE LUNCH WITCH #1

Scarlett
Star on the Run

SCARLETT

ANNE of GREEN BAGELS
Susan Schade
Jon Buller

ANNE OF GREEN BAGELS #1

DRACULA MARRIES FRANKENSTEIN!
Susan Schade
Jon Buller

DRACULA MARRIES FRANKENSTEIN!

THE RED SHOES AND OTHER TALES
METAPHROG

THE RED SHOES

The Little Mermaid
METAPHROG

THE LITTLE MERMAID

JOHN STEVEN GURNEY
Fuzzy Baseball

FUZZY BASEBALL
COMING SOON

The Sisters

THE SISTERS #1

The Sisters

THE SISTERS #2

The Sisters

THE SISTERS #3

The Sisters

THE SISTERS #4

THE SUPER SISTERS

SUPER SISTERS

THE SMURFS, THE GARFIELD SHOW, BARBIE, and TROLLS graphic novels are available for $7.99 in paperback, and $12.99 in hardcover. GERONIMO STILTON and THEA STILTON graphic novels are available for $9.99 in hardcover only. FUZZY BASEBALL and NANCY DREW DIAR graphic novels are available for $9.99 in paperback only. THE LUNCH WITCH, SCARLETT, and ANNE OF GREEN BAGELS graphic novels are available for $14.99 in paperback only. THE RED SHOES graphic novel is available for $12.99 in hardcover only. Available from booksellers everywhere. You can also order online from www.papercutz.com. Or call 1-800-886-1223, Monday through Friday, 9 EST. MC, Visa, and AmEx accepted. To order by mail, please add $5.00 for postage and handling for first book ordered, $1.00 for each additic book and make check payable to NBM Publishing. Send to: Papercutz, 160 Broadway, Suite 700, East Wing, New York, NY 10038.

THE SMURFS, THE GARFIELD SHOW, BARBIE, TROLLS, GERONIMO STILTON, THEA STILTON, FUZZY BASEBALL, THE LUNCH WITCH, NANCY DREW DIARIES, THE RED SHOES, ANNE OF GREEN BAGELS, and SCARLETT graphic novels are also available wherever e-books are sold.

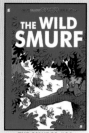

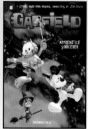

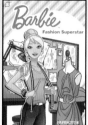

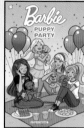

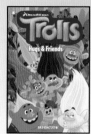

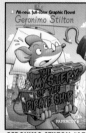

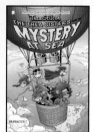

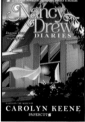

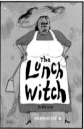

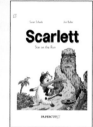

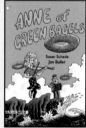

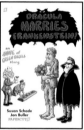

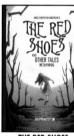

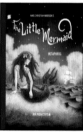

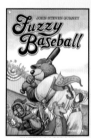

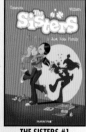

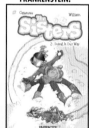

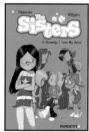

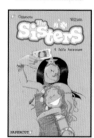

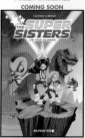

4: "Selfie Awareness"

Art and colors
William

Story
Cazenove & William

PAPERCUT*Z*

New York

To our friends in Sète!
To Wendy and Marine ("Maureen"),
my two adored tornadoes who are
always so hard on my pencils.

Marine: *Say, Wendy, why does*
Daddy say there are two-doored
tornadoes in his studio?
Wendy: *LOL, well, I think it's*
actually a metaphor.
Marine: *A what?*
Wendy: *Let it go. He's just saying*
that he loves us. That's all!

Thank you to Olivier Sulpice
and his fine team, and props to
Mister Christopher "Hot Gag Brain"
Cazenove.

THE SISTERS #4 "Selfie Awareness"
Les Sisters [The Sisters] by Cazenove and William
© 2012, 2013 Bamboo Édition
Sisters, characters and related indicia are copyright, trademark and
exclusive license of Bamboo Édition.
English translation and all other editorial material © 2017 by Papercutz.
All rights reserved.

Story by Cazenove and William
Art and color by William
Cover by William
Translation by Nanette McGuinness
Lettering by Wilson Ramos Jr.

For information address
Bamboo Édition:
116, rue des Jonchères –
BP 3, 71012 CHARNAY-lès-MÂCON cedex FRANCE
bamboo@bamboo.fr – www.bamboo.fr

Papercutz books may be purchased for business or promotional use.
For information on bulk purchases please contact Macmillan
Corporate and Premium Sales Department at
(800) 221-7945 x5442

Production – Dawn Guzzo
Assistant Managing Editor – Jeff Whitman
Jim Salicrup
Editor-in-Chief

PB ISBN: 978-1-62991-799-3
HC ISBN: 978-1-62991-798-6

Printed in China
November 2017

Distributed by Macmillan
First Papercutz Printing

EVEN WHEN SHE WAS LITTLE, MAUREEN LOVED HUGS...

COME GIVE WENDY A HUG.

"DEEDEE."

YESSS. JUST THREE MORE LITTLE STEPS.

"STEHPS."

CLINK TINK

OOHOOH, SHE REALLY LOVES HER BIG SISTER!

"THISTER."

YOU JUST CAN'T DO WITHOUT ME, ISN'T THAT SO?

"ATSO."

AH AH AH... YOU LOVE HUGS!

"UVHUGS."

AND THEN ONE DAY I FIGURED IT OUT...

ARE YOU COMING TO GIVE ME A BIG HUG?

INTO MY ARMS, MAUREEN.

THERRRRE. THAT'S GREAT, MAUR--

GAGA.

...THE HARSH REALITY...

...IT WASN'T ME SHE WAS INTERESTED IN...

...IT WAS THE ARMCHAIR!

PFFF...

CAZENOVE et WILLIAM

5

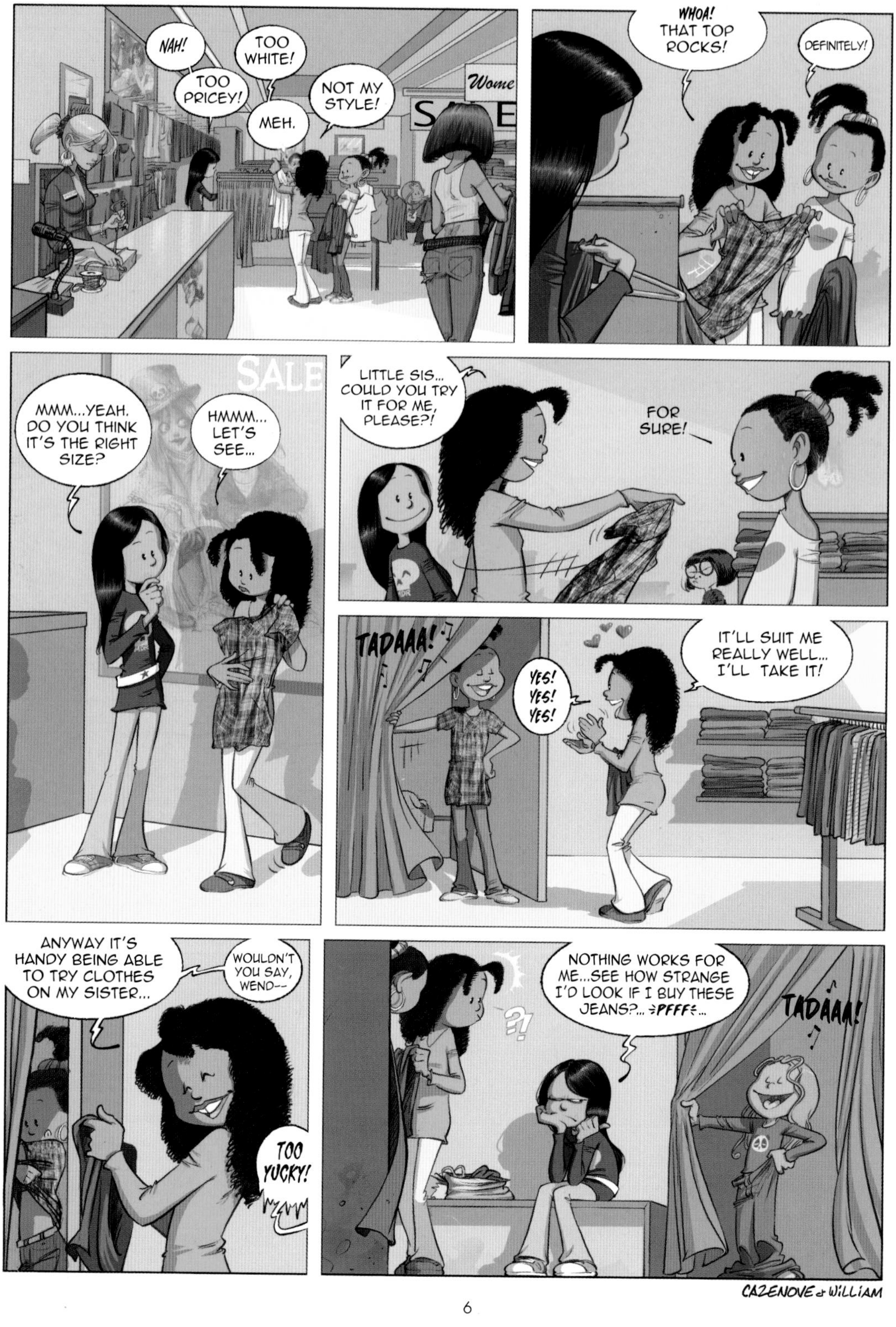
NAH!
TOO PRICEY!
TOO WHITE!
MEH.
NOT MY STYLE!
Wome
SALE
WHOA! THAT TOP ROCKS!
DEFINITELY!
SALE
MMM...YEAH. DO YOU THINK IT'S THE RIGHT SIZE?
HMMM... LET'S SEE...
LITTLE SIS... COULD YOU TRY IT FOR ME, PLEASE?!
FOR SURE!
TADAAA!
YES! YES! YES!
IT'LL SUIT ME REALLY WELL... I'LL TAKE IT!
ANYWAY IT'S HANDY BEING ABLE TO TRY CLOTHES ON MY SISTER...
WOULDN'T YOU SAY, WEND--
TOO YUCKY!
?!
NOTHING WORKS FOR ME...SEE HOW STRANGE I'D LOOK IF I BUY THESE JEANS?... PFFF...
TADAAA!
CAZENOVE & WILLIAM

LULU AND I PLANTED STRAWBERRIES TOGETHER...YUM!

THEY NEED PAMPERING...

WE TOOK PROPER CARE OF THEM...

THEY'RE VERY THIRSTY!

TOTALLY.

I FERTILIZED THEM THE WAY DADDY TOLD ME TO...

WE PULLED THE BAD WEEDS...

JEEPERS! NASTY DOGTOOTH VIOLET!

I TOSSED OUT THE CREEPY CRAWLIES AND ALL THAT...

GO AWAY! GO PLAY SOMEWHERE ELSE!

FLICK

BUT EVEN SO, NO STRAWBERRIES EVER GREW...

SHOOT!

I DON'T THINK THIS ONE'S GOING TO GROW...

OUT YOU GO! WE'LL REPLACE YOU!

LUCKILY, I'VE GOT LOTS OF OTHER BRAND NEW ONES.

MAYBE WE SHOULD WAIT MORE THAN TEN MINUTES BEFORE PULLING IT OUT THIS TIME?!

WHAT WOULD YOU SAY? A HALF HOUR?!

CAZENOVE et WILLIAM

7

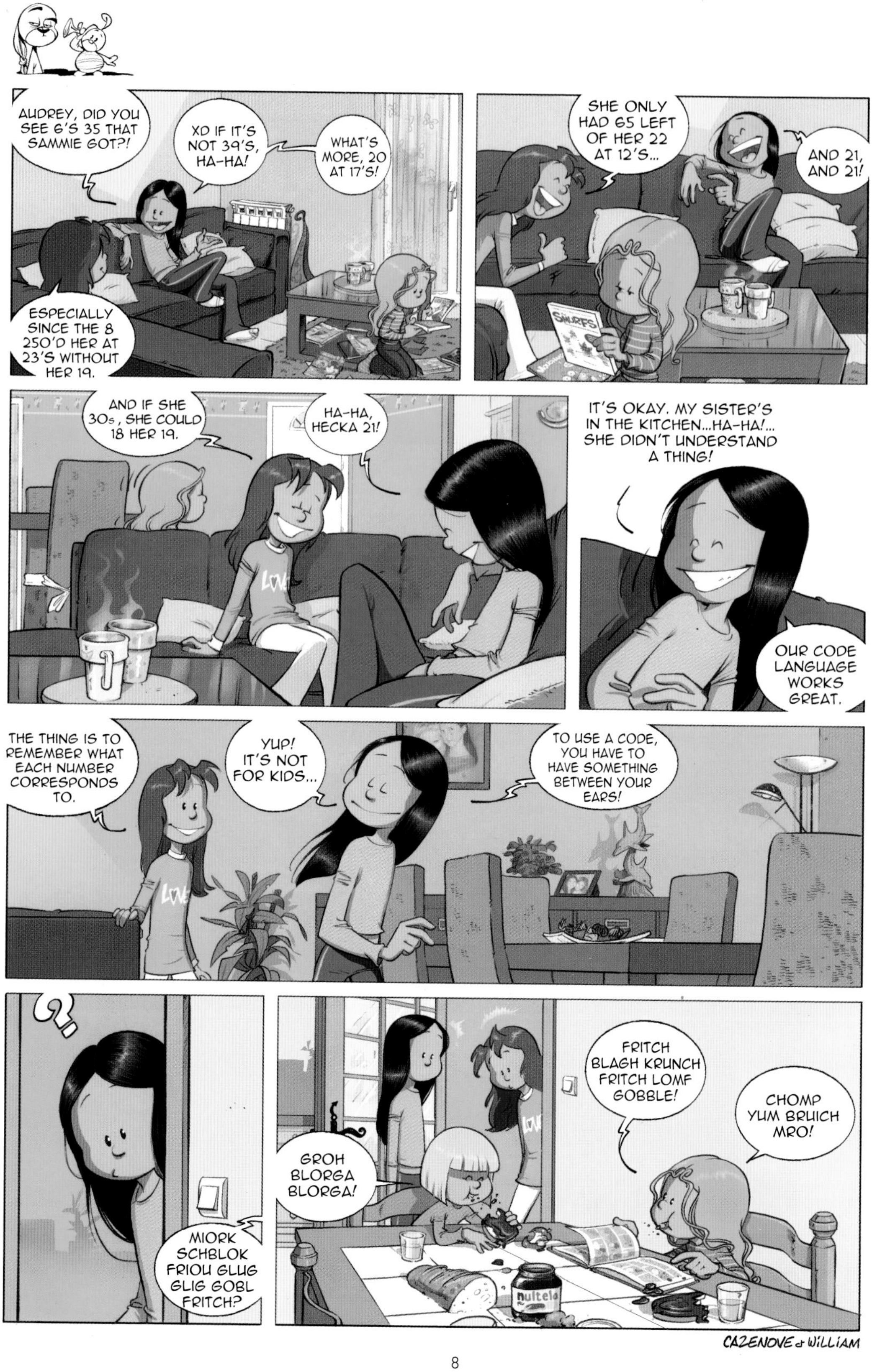
AUDREY, DID YOU SEE 6'S 35 THAT SAMMIE GOT?!
XD IF IT'S NOT 39'S, HA-HA!
WHAT'S MORE, 20 AT 17'S!
ESPECIALLY SINCE THE 8 250'D HER AT 23'S WITHOUT HER 19.
SHE ONLY HAD 65 LEFT OF HER 22 AT 12'S...
AND 21, AND 21!
AND IF SHE 30s, SHE COULD 18 HER 19.
HA-HA, HECKA 21!
IT'S OKAY. MY SISTER'S IN THE KITCHEN...HA-HA!... SHE DIDN'T UNDERSTAND A THING!
OUR CODE LANGUAGE WORKS GREAT.
THE THING IS TO REMEMBER WHAT EACH NUMBER CORRESPONDS TO.
YUP! IT'S NOT FOR KIDS...
TO USE A CODE, YOU HAVE TO HAVE SOMETHING BETWEEN YOUR EARS!
?
MIORK SCHBLOK FRIOU GLUG GLIG GOBL FRITCH?
GROH BLORGA BLORGA!
FRITCH BLAGH KRUNCH FRITCH LOMF GOBBLE!
CHOMP YUM BRUICH MRO!
CAZENOVE & WILLIAM

THAT'S MY HALLOWEEN COSTUME?

YOU ARE TOO CUTE. YOU LOOK LIKE A FAIRY QUEEN.

ARE YOU NUTS OR WHAT? MY WINGS ARE BADMINTON RACKETS.

I LOOK LIKE THE LOSER QUEEN INSTEAD.

ALRIGHT, ALREADY. LET'S CHANGE. I'VE GOT THIS COVERED. TRY THIS.

I LOOK LIKE AN IDIOT IN THIS!

AH, NO! I REALLY LOOK STUPID IN THIS ONE!

THE DUMBEST OF DUMB!

HATE IT!

NAAA...THIS IS TOTALLY CHEESY!

AH-HA! I'VE GOT AN IDEA!

WOOW! YOUR CHEESE COSTUME'S SO GREAT, MAUREEN!

YUP, I KNOW!

AND I'M THE ONE WHO THOUGHT OF IT!

CAZENOVE et WILLIAM

9

UH...SORRY I'M LATE, WENDY...

...BUT... I HAD TO CLEAN UP MY ROOM!

DON'T WORRY, *SAMMIE!* I'VE HAD THAT HAPPEN, TOO.

BUT NOT ANYMORE?

I FOUND A WAY TO GET PAST THAT CHORE AT THE SPEED OF LIGHT.

NO KIDDING?!

TELL ME. I'M UP FOR IT.

IT'S A WHOLE TECHNIQUE...

STEP 1: COLLECT EVERYTHING THAT'S LYING AROUND...

AND PRESTO! I MOVE IT ALL UNDER MY BED.

AND MOST OF ALL, THERE'S ANOTHER ADVANTAGE THAT'S PRETTY SIGNIFICANT...

WHAT'S THAT?

WHEN I'M NOT THERE AND MY SISTER WANTS TO RUMMAGE ALL AROUND...

THERE'S NO LONGER ANY WAY FOR HER TO HIDE WHEN I COME BACK UNEXPECTEDLY.

HAHA!

LOL! THAT'S SO GREAT!

CAZENOVE et WILLIAM

WENDY... IT'S READY! WE'RE SITTING DOWN TO EAT!

YES, YES, I'M COMING!

CAREFUL, MAUREEN, IT'S VERY HOT!

YUM! I LOVE THIS.

HA-HA! AND YOU MISSED THAT PART...

HA-HA! THAT'S TOO FUNNY!

DINNER'S SERRRRRVED!

THAT ONE'S MY FAVORITE.

BWAH-HA-HA... I LOOOVE IT... CRAZY...

IT'S WARM!

STRAIGHT FROM FACEBOOK!

HEH HEH, CHECK THIS ONE OUT! ⸙MWARF!⸙

TOO MUCH!

HEE HEE! WHAT AN IDIOT!

IT'S COLD!

WELL, I'M HEADED IN! OTHERWISE SHE'LL KEEP FREAKING OUT!

EAT UP!

IT'S TOOOO LAAATE!

CAZENOVE et WILLIAM

11

GIRLS...FOR THE LAST TIME, *DINNNNER'S SERVED!*

TOO TOO TOOLOO ♪ ♫ TWEET TWEET TOOLOO TOOT

YES, MOM. TWO MINUTES. I'LL SAVE MY GAME.

?

THERE. IT'S SAVED.

CLICK

WENDY, WHAT DOES "SAVE GAME" MEAN?

WELL, SINCE I CAN'T FINISH UP NOW BECAUSE WE HAVE TO GO TO DINNER, I SAVE IT...

UH...

I PUT IT TO THE SIDE, SO THAT I CAN PLAY IT LATER...FOR WHEN I HAVE TIME FOR IT.

AH, OKAY!

OH, NOOOO... BOILED VEGETABLES... GROSS!

EWWWW! YUCK!

MOMMY, SAVE MY VEGETABLES. I'LL DEAL WITH THEM LATER... WHEN I HAVE TIME.

CAZENOVE et WILLIAM

12

OH, NO! THE SLAM HAS ALREADY STARTED ?!

JUST THIS MINUTE!

KILLER BABE'S MY FAVORITE!

SHE'S SO GREAT!

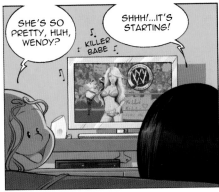

SHE'S SO PRETTY, HUH, WENDY?

SHH!...IT'S STARTING!

♪ KILLER BABE ♪

HER SPECIALTY IS NECK WRINGING...

AND SHE FOLLOWS THAT UP WITH--

UH-UH-UH! I KNOW ALL THE BIG BOMBER'S HOLDS BY HEART...

AH AH

OW! NO FAIR! OUUUUCHH!

THERE! A SCHNOZZ PINCHAGE!

THE TAG-TEAM TACKLE.

REVENGE!

NO FAIR! I'M ON THE ROPES.

BOP BOP

ULTIMATE POWER SLAM!

GNII

THUMP

KILLER! KILLER!

WE'RE PROFESSIONALS, DON'T TRY THIS AT HOME!

WATCH OUT!

DANGER

YOU

?!

AH, WELL, HEY! THAT'S SNEAKY. CAN SOMEBODY EXPLAIN WHY...

THEY COULDN'T SAY THAT *BEFORE* THE FIGHTS!

CAZENOVE et WILLIAM

13

THAT'S THE 50TH TIME I'VE TOLD YOU! WE REALLY CAN'T TRUST YOU.

UH-OH. RED ZONE. THINGS ARE HEATING UP OVER THERE.

I'M SORRY, MOM. I FORGOT.

WELL, NOW, AS FOR FORGETTING...

AS USUAL, WHENEVER WE TELL YOU SOMETHING IT GOES IN ONE EAR AND OUT THE OTHER!

SO THAT'S WHY!

YOU'RE GROUNDED!

YES!

MAUREEEEN... YOU DIDN'T CLEAN UP YOUR ROOOOOOOM... HEY, UP THERE... YOU DO HEAR ME, RIGHT? MAUREEEEN...

THIS WAY, I CAN BE SURE I'LL NEVER AGAIN FORGET SOMETHING MOM TELLS ME.

I'M SO AWESOME!

14

CAZENOVE et WILLIAM

WRESTLING TIME!

BLAM! FUJIWARA ARMBAR SMASH!

NECK WRINGING.

AND **CRACK!** LUMBAR CHECK!

HA! BACK-BREAKING BEAR HUG!

WOO! I'M SUPER-MEGA-READY.

I'M THE "QUEEN OF THE RING!"

IT'S **PAYBACK** TIME, MISS IMINCHARGEHERE...

ATTACK!

AAAHH... BUT UH...NO FAAAIIIR!

THAT'S NOT A LEGAL **WRESTLING** HOLD....!

CAZENOVE et WILLIAM

15

ARGH!...MAUREEN, ARE THOSE MY EARRINGS YOU'RE WEARING THERE?!

WELLCH, YOUCH NEVERCH TOLCH MEECH THACH I COULDN'TCH WEARCH THEMCH...

:MUNCH:

TAKE THEM OFF RIGHT NOOOW! YOU LITTLE THIEF!

PLUS, THESE WERE A PRESENT FROM MASON...

IF I'M NOT WEARING THEM HE'S GOING TO THINK I DON'T LIKE HIM.

BOYS ARE SO SENSITIVE.

AAAH... BUT AAAAH!

NOT WITH YOUR FINGERS ALL STINKY WITH CHEESE... AAAH!

BRAVO! WELL PLAYED...

I'LL HAVE TO SOAK THEM IN BLEACH NOW!

GRUMBLE

YOU WERE RIGHT, LULU!

YES, HEE HEE!

SHE WAS SO FOCUSED ON HER EARRINGS THAT SHE DIDN'T EVEN NOTICE I'M WEARING HER FAVORITE SWEATSHIRT.

CAZENOVE et WILLIAM

16

WENDY, I CAN'T TIE THE KNOT ON RAPUNZEL'S DRESS...

SHOW ME HOW, PRETTY PLEASE?

OKAY! COME OVER HERE.

...GET IT? YOU SLIP THE RIBBON THROUGH THE LOOP AND TIGHTEN IT.

BUT NOT TOO TIGHT OR ELSE IT WILL BE UGLY.

WOOW!

YOU'RE SO GREAT!

AND I HAVE SOMETHING I DIDN'T UNDERSTAND IN MATH CLASS...CAN YOU EXPLAIN IT TO ME?

COOL! I LOVE MATH PROBLEMS!

YOU BREAK DOWN THE CALCULATION, SEE? FIRST YOU ADD AND THEN YOU SUBTRACT.

YOU SO ROCK. YOU'RE SO SMART.

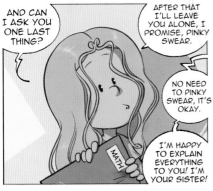

AND CAN I ASK YOU ONE LAST THING?

AFTER THAT I'LL LEAVE YOU ALONE, I PROMISE, PINKY SWEAR.

NO NEED TO PINKY SWEAR, IT'S OKAY.

I'M HAPPY TO EXPLAIN EVERYTHING TO YOU! I'M YOUR SISTER!

COULD YOU TEACH ME HOW TO KNIT?

UH...

...I'LL SHOW YOU THIS AFTERNOON, PROMISE.

...I'VE GOT SOMETHING URGENT TO DO FIRST.

OKAY! YOU'RE FANTASTIC!

MOM, WOULD YOU TEACH ME HOW TO KNIT, PLEASE?

AND FAIRLY SOON...I'VE GOT A REPUTATION TO MAINTAIN, YOU KNOW.

CAZENOVE et WILLIAM

17

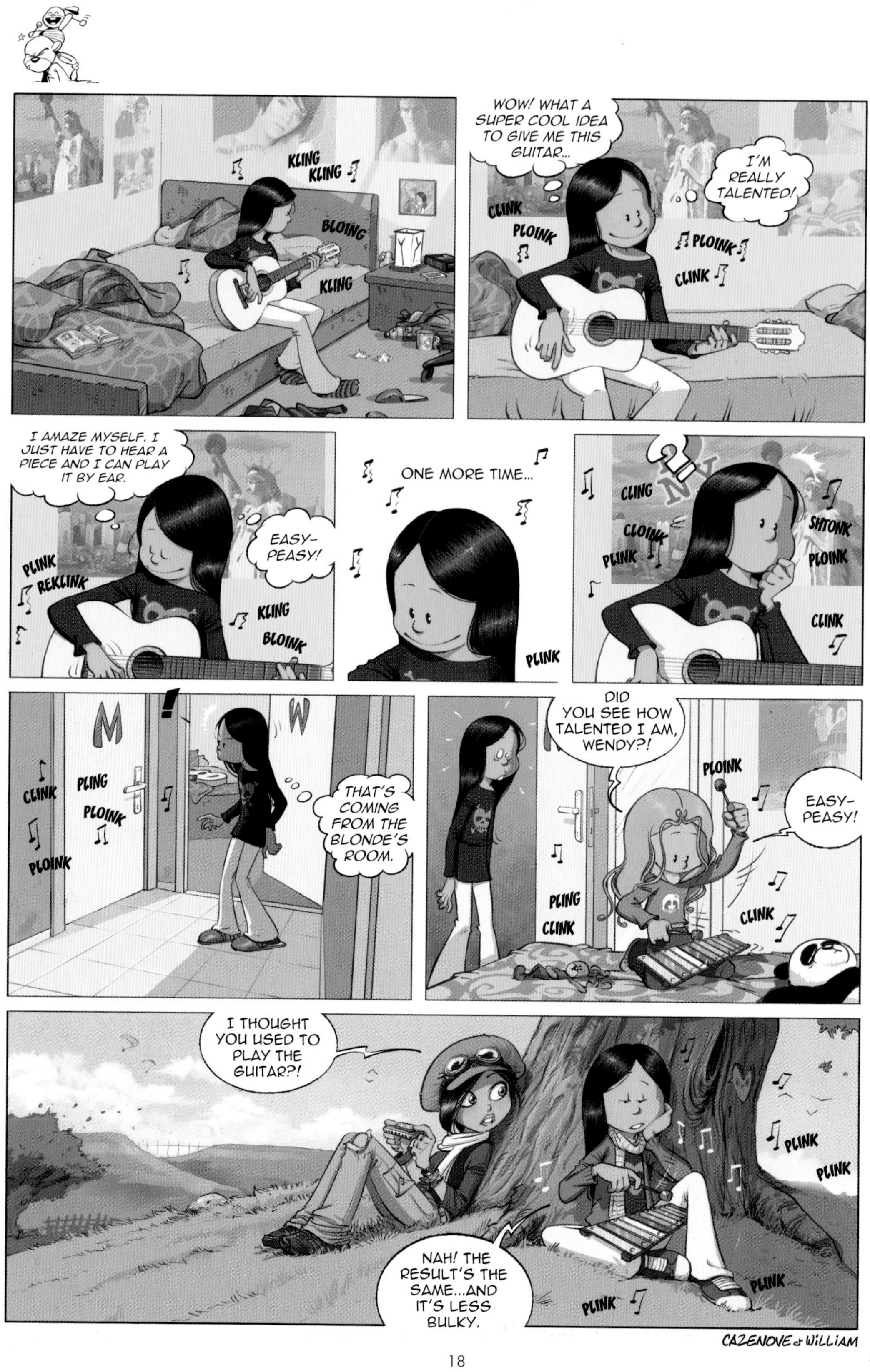
KLING
KLING
BLOING
KLING
WOW! WHAT A SUPER COOL IDEA TO GIVE ME THIS GUITAR...
I'M REALLY TALENTED!
CLINK
PLOINK
PLOINK
CLINK
I AMAZE MYSELF. I JUST HAVE TO HEAR A PIECE AND I CAN PLAY IT BY EAR.
EASY-PEASY!
PLINK
REKLINK
KLING
BLOINK
ONE MORE TIME...
PLINK
CLING
CLOINK
PLINK
SHTONK
PLOINK
CLINK
M
!
W
CLINK
PLING
PLOINK
PLOINK
THAT'S COMING FROM THE BLONDE'S ROOM.
DID YOU SEE HOW TALENTED I AM, WENDY?!
PLOINK
EASY-PEASY!
PLING
CLINK
CLINK
I THOUGHT YOU USED TO PLAY THE GUITAR?!
PLINK
PLINK
NAH! THE RESULT'S THE SAME...AND IT'S LESS BULKY.
PLINK
PLINK

CAZENOVE & WILLIAM

PARA BRAILLAR
MABAMBA...
PARA BRAILLAR
MABAMBA
CLINK CLINK
CLONK
CLONK

SHTOING
?!

OH, RATS!
I BROKE A
STRING.

WENDY'S
GOING TO
TAR AND
FEATHER ME!

I THINK I SAW
SOME STRINGS IN
DADDY'S STUDIO...

SZZM

YES!
SAVED!

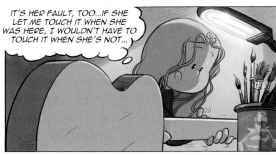
IT'S HER FAULT, TOO...IF SHE
LET ME TOUCH IT WHEN SHE
WAS HERE, I WOULDN'T HAVE TO
TOUCH IT WHEN SHE'S NOT...

HEY, THERE!
ANYBODY HOME?

YIKES!
SHE'S
ALREADY
COME
BACK!

MAUREEEEN...YOU
TOUCHED MY GUITAAAAAAR
AGAIN AND ON TOP OF
THAT YOU BROKE A
STRING...GAAH!

WELL...I...I...DON'T
KNOW WHAT YOU'RE
TALKING ABOUT...ALL
YOUR STRINGS ARE
THERE, RIGHT?!

CAZENOVE et WILLIAM

19

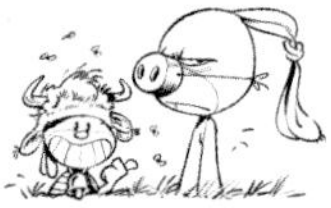

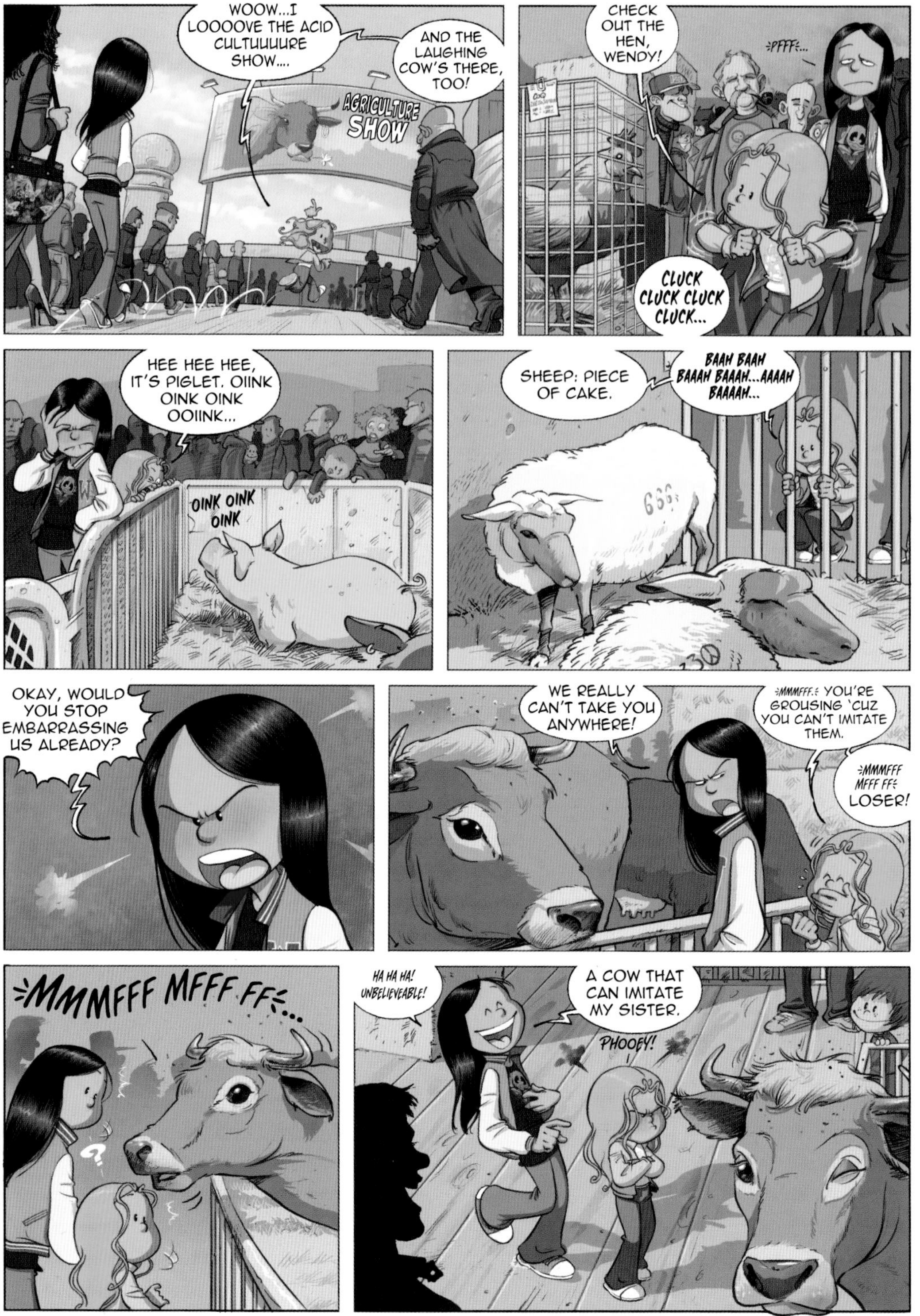
WOOW...I LOOOOVE THE ACID CULTUUUURE SHOW....
AND THE LAUGHING COW'S THERE, TOO!
AGRICULTURE SHOW
CHECK OUT THE HEN, WENDY!
PFFF...
CLUCK CLUCK CLUCK CLUCK...
HEE HEE HEE, IT'S PIGLET. OIIINK OINK OINK OOIINK...
OINK OINK OINK
SHEEP: PIECE OF CAKE.
BAAH BAAH BAAAH BAAAH...AAAAH BAAAAH...
OKAY, WOULD YOU STOP EMBARRASSING US ALREADY?
WE REALLY CAN'T TAKE YOU ANYWHERE!
MMMFFF... YOU'RE GROUSING 'CUZ YOU CAN'T IMITATE THEM.
MMMFFF MFFF FF... LOSER!
MMMFFF MFFF FF...
?
HA HA HA! UNBELIEVEABLE!
A COW THAT CAN IMITATE MY SISTER.
PHOOEY!

CAZENOVE & WILLIAM

WENDY, WHERE'RE WE GOING ON VACATION ALREADY?

WHY.

WHY? CUZ I WANT TO KNOW. THAT'S WHY!

WE ARE HEADED TO WHY! MOM AND DAD EXPLAINED THIS.

UH...

ARE YOU DOING THIS ON PURPOSE OR DO YOU PRACTICE?

WHY AREN'T YOU TELLING ME?! YOU AREN'T EXPLAINING! YOU'RE REALLY MEAN!

OH, COME ON! OKAY, FOR THE LAST TIME...DAD, MOM, YOU AND I ARE LEAVING FOR WHY. IT'S A SMALL RESORT TOWN. IS THAT CLEAR?

YES, YES. BUT WHERE ARE WE GOING?

ARRGHH!... SHE'S SUCH A PAIN. SHE'S SUCH A PAIN! AIEEEE!

UMM, MOMMY. CAN'T WE GO ON VACATION SOMEWHERE ELSE?

BECAUSE I UNDERSTAND WHY, BUT I STILL DON'T KNOW WHERE...

CAZENOVE et WILLIAM

21

I STILL DON'T KNOW WHERE WE ARE. I WANTED TO STAY WITH MY FRIEND LULU.

WHY

SPENDING VACATION AT A PORT IS TOTALLY AWESOME, DON'T YOU THINK?

NO! I DON'T LIKE THE WATER!

BUT YOU LIKE THE SEA, THOUGH!

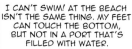

I CAN'T SWIM! AT THE BEACH ISN'T THE SAME THING. MY FEET CAN TOUCH THE BOTTOM, BUT NOT IN A PORT THAT'S FILLED WITH WATER.

I DON'T LIKE WATER IN PORTS THAT'S TOO DEEP.

IS THAT CLEAR?!

WHATEVS!

IN ANY CASE, I'M GOING TO HAVE A BLAST AND SUNBATHE ON ALAN'S BOAT, MOM'S FRIEND'S DAD.

A BOAT?!

I LOOOVE BOATS!

THEY'RE SO PRETTY. THEY'RE SO CUTE!

WHERE IS IT?

WHERE IS IT?

HEY, AHOY, MAUREEN

NO! YOU'RE PULLING MY LEG...

THIS BOAT'S SITTING IN THE MIDDLE OF WATER!

CAZENOVE et WILLIAM

22

ALAN, YOUR BOAT'S *SO CUTE.*

WILL I BE ABLE TO ROW?

HEH HEH... NO NEED TO ROW IN THIS TYPE OF BOAT, HONEY.

OH, YEAH? RATS, THEN!

I KNOW, I KNOW, I'LL TAKE CARE OF THE SALES, LIKE AT A CASH REGISTER.

NO SAILS EITHER, MY LITTLE MAUREEN.

I CAN FIND NORTH FOR YOU. WHEN I GO MUSHROOM HUNTING WITH WENDY, I ALWAYS CAN FIND IT.

SORRY, BUT YOU KNOW I'VE ALREADY GOT MY COMPASS, WHICH TAKES CARE OF IT.

≈PFFF≈... IT'S STUPID! IF I CAN'T HELP IT'S NOT A REAL VACATION THEN.

I MIGHT HAVE SOMETHING FOR YOU...

YOU CAN CLEAN MY FISHING NETS...

THIS ONE REALLY NEEDS IT.

COME ON! I'M NOT HERE TO DO WORK...

I'M ON *VACATION!*

CAZENOVE et WILLIAM

23

AND HERE WE HAVE THE DEPTH GAUGE.

OR, MORE SIMPLY, A FISH RADAR.

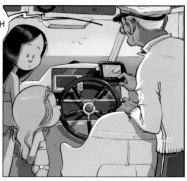

UH, ALAN...WHEN MAUREEN MAKES THAT FACE, IT MEANS SHE HASN'T UNDERSTOOD A THING.

OH, YEAH?

SHE'S FLOUNDERING EVEN MORE!

LOOK, HONEY, IT WORKS USING THE SAME PRINCIPLE AS SONAR.

IT'S LIKE ECHOES IN THE MOUNTAINS...

HAVE YOU HEARD ECHOES BEFORE?!

APRIL

IT'S LIKE A PHOTO OF WHAT'S THERE UNDER THE WATER, IF YOU WILL...

I GET IT NOW!

YAHOO!

BUT WHY DID SHE JUMP IN?

LOL! SHE ALWAYS WANTS TO BE IN EVERY PHOTO!

YOO HOO!

CAZENOVE et WILLIAM

YOU HEARD DAD...EACH OF US EATS THE STEAMERS SHE COLLECTS.

HERE'S YOUR PAIL.

BUUU STEAM? I DON'T EVEN SEE ANY STEAM!

HA-HA! THAT MEANS SHELLFISH, SHRIMP, CRABS, AND ALL THAT.

TOO COOL! I LOVE IT! I'M GOING TO FISH IT FULL OF SURIMI, TOO!

I HAVE A HECKA TECHNIQUE! I'M GOING TO EAT TONS OF THEM TONIGHT!

HELLO, THERE, LITTLE MUSSEL...WOULD YOU LIKE TO COME WITH M--

OWWWWWW!

OWIIEE!

OUCH!

OWWW!

OWWW!

I REALLY HAVE TO ADMIT IT...

MMMM... SEAFOOD IS SOOO GOOD.

HERE YOU GO, SWEETHEART. YOU REALLY EARNED IT.

...HER "TECHNIQUE" IS HECKA GOOD!

CAZENOVE et WILLIAM

HEE HEE, YOUR PJ LOOK IS TOO WEIRD!

IT'S A DIVING SUIT, DUMMY!

OH, YEAHHHHH... YOU'RE STILL DOING THAT. EVEN THOUGH I WOULD HAVE LOVED TO SO MUCH!

ANYWAY, YOU'RE TOO LITTLE. YOU WON'T BE ABLE TO DO IT.

HOW MANY ZILLIONS DO YOU WANT TO BET?

I CAN DO EVERYTHING YOU CAN, JUST LIKE YOU AND BETTER, SO THERE!

BESIDES THERE AREN'T ANY SUITS IN YOUR SIZE...

I DON'T NEED YOUR FANCY CLOTHING TO GO IN THE WATER!

PROOF THAT I'M A BIG GIRL!

AS YOU WISH...

LET'S DO IT! OFF I GO!

PREPARE TO BE AMAZED! IT'S MAUREEN THE MERMAID, SO MAKE WAY, HERE SHE COMES! YAY!

ARE YOU KIDDING ME? I TOLD YOU SO!

YOU'RE TOO MUCH OF A BABY TO GO DIVING!

I'LL GET THERE! I'LL GET THERE!

CAZENOVE et WILLIAM

26

AND I'LL GET THAT ONE, TOO, PLUS THE BIG ONE...

AND I WANT THAT WEIRD, CUT-OUT ONE UP THERE, TOO.

I ❤ WHY

POSTCARDS

I CAN'T WAIT TO FILL THEM OUT, WOOW!

≥PHEW.≤ IT'S HOT...

WANT TO GO SWIMMING, MAUREEN?

NAH! I'M BUSY HERE.

MISSION ACCOMPLISHED! I'VE FINISHED ALL OF THEM.

SO AWESOME!

WHY

HEY, YOU REALLY SPOIL YOUR BUDS.

MAIL

THESE AREN'T FOR THEM!

THEY'RE FOR OUR COUSINS?!

DADDY AND MOMMY?!

GRANDMA LENOU?!

NOPE. ALL WRONG!

THEY'RE ALL FOR ME...

I'LL NEED TO KNOW WHETHER I'VE HAD A NICE VACATION, RIGHT?

CAZENOVE et WILLIAM

27

SOMETIMES VILLAINS AREN'T VERY CLEVER...

HEY, YOUR DEVIL FROM THE UNDERWORLD HITS LIKE A GIRL.

WHAT A FOOL!

THEY'RE ALWAYS FORGETTING WE CAN'T BE HURT AT ALL.

AND THEIR COMPANION DOGS AREN'T ANY BETTER.

BARELY TICKLES!

THEY DON'T GET THAT WE'RE UNDERGOING A TRIAL BY FIRE...

WHAT A BUNCH OF DUMMIES!

WOW! THIS LAVA'S TOO COOL. IT'LL CLEAN OFF OUR BOOTS.

WE FEAR NEITHER FLAMES NOR HEAT... WE EMBRACE THEM INSTEAD...

I'LL ATOMIZE THE WITCH!

OKAY, I'LL TAKE CARE OF THE EMBERS.

THERE, WE'VE THRASHED EVERYONE!

UH...

WHAT'S THAT?

? ? ?

BUT THAT SUMMER, WE WERE FELLED BY A REAL TOUGHIE.

YUP, THE WHY SUN SURE PACKS A PUNCH!

TOTALLY! IT'S NO JOKE!

CAZENOVE et WILLIAM

28

WENDY, COME SEE HOW PRETTY THIS IS!

CLICK

I'M COMING. I'M JUST FINISHING TAKING THESE PICTURES TO SEND THEM TO SAMMIE.

CLICK

PLEASE CURB YOUR DOG. DOGGY DOO BAGS

DON'T YOU THINK YOU COULD TAKE SOME PRETTIER ONES?!

LOOK AROUND YOU. IT'S REALLY SPLENDID.

CLICK

DON'T YOU WANT TO MAKE HER HAPPY BY SENDING HER PRETTY PICTURES?

OF COURSE...

...SHE *IS* MY BEST BUD.

CLICK

BUT HERE'S THE STORY...

CLICK

THIS SUMMER, SAMMIE ISN'T GOING ON VACATION...

SO I DON'T WANT TO MAKE HER FEEL JEALOUS.

CAZENOVE et WILLIAM

29

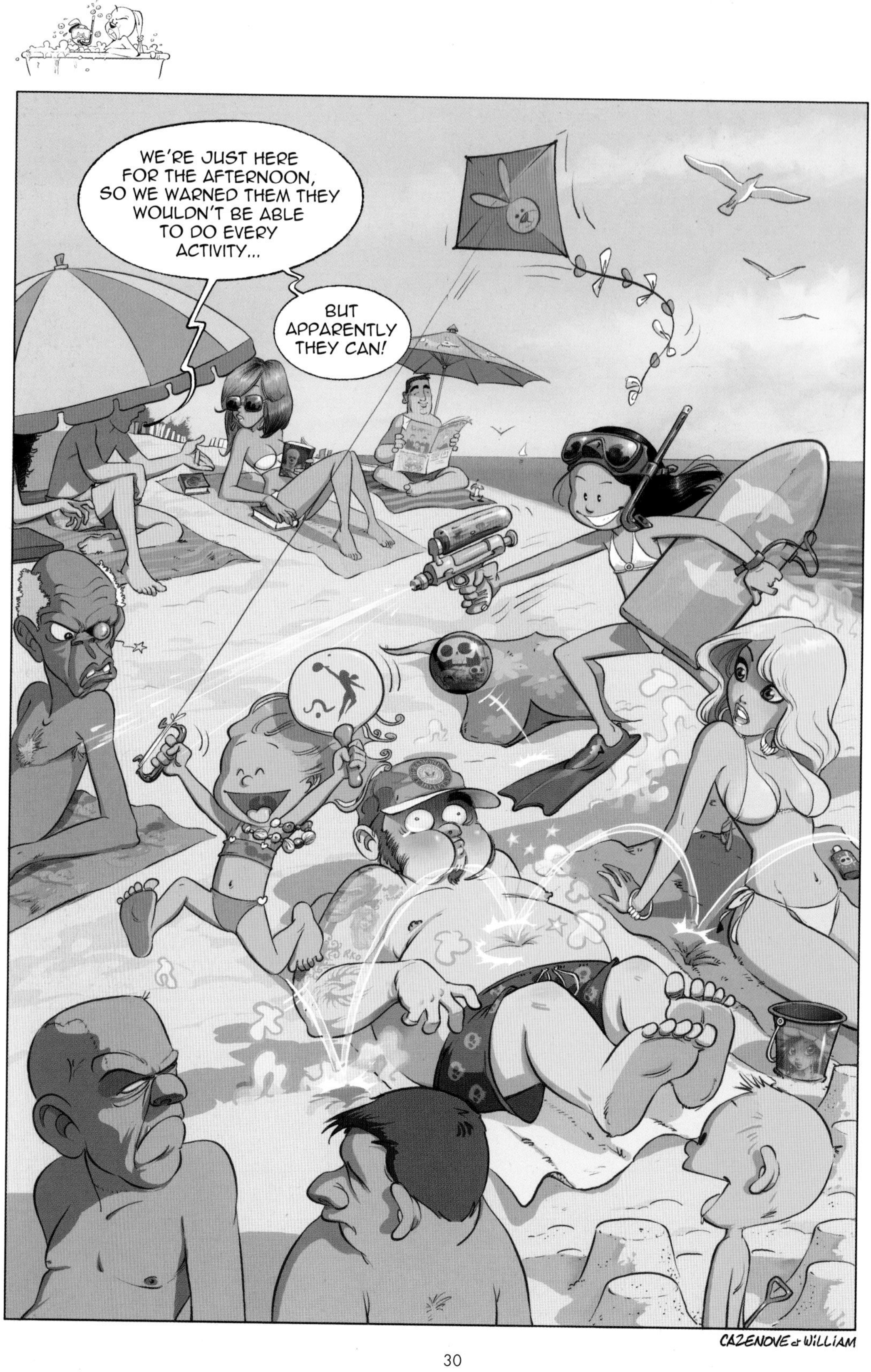
WE'RE JUST HERE FOR THE AFTERNOON, SO WE WARNED THEM THEY WOULDN'T BE ABLE TO DO EVERY ACTIVITY...
BUT APPARENTLY THEY CAN!
CAZENOVE & WILLIAM

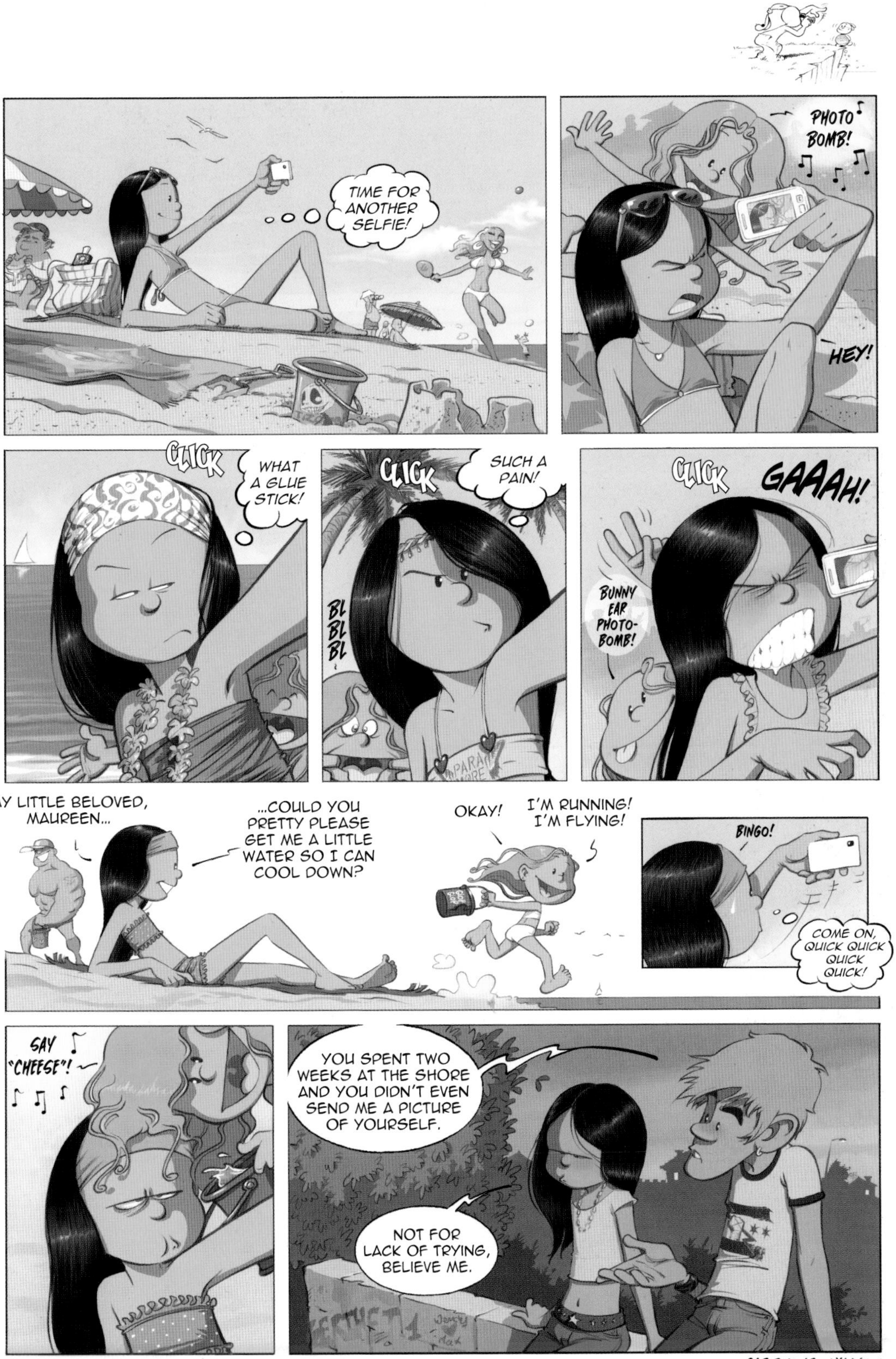

TIME FOR ANOTHER SELFIE!
PHOTO BOMB!
HEY!
CLICK
WHAT A GLUE STICK!
CLICK
SUCH A PAIN!
BL BL BL
CLICK
GAAAH!
BUNNY EAR PHOTO-BOMB!
MY LITTLE BELOVED, MAUREEN...
...COULD YOU PRETTY PLEASE GET ME A LITTLE WATER SO I CAN COOL DOWN?
OKAY!
I'M RUNNING! I'M FLYING!
BINGO!
COME ON, QUICK QUICK QUICK QUICK!
SAY "CHEESE"!
YOU SPENT TWO WEEKS AT THE SHORE AND YOU DIDN'T EVEN SEND ME A PICTURE OF YOURSELF.
NOT FOR LACK OF TRYING, BELIEVE ME.
CAZENOVE & WILLIAM

HEY, WENDY AND MAUREEN HAVE COME BACK FROM VACATION...

WOW! DID YOU SEE THAT?! IT'S CRAZY!

I'M SO JEEEEEALOUS... YOU'RE SO TAN, GIRLS!

TOTALLY!

YOOHOO...!

TWO WEEKS BASKING IN THE SUN ON THE BEACH.

HEE HEE! WE STOLE THE SUNRAYS FROM EVERYONE, EH, WENDY?!

BUT ANYWAY I'M THE MOST TANNED, RIGHT?

I'D SAY YOU WIN THE MEDAL THERE.

RESPECT!

SO WHO'S THE TANNEST OF THE LAND?

≥PFFF.≤ BARELY. PLUS IT'S A BLONDE SUNTAN.

DON'T BE SUCH A SHOW-OFF! YOU SPENT MORE TIME IN THE SUN THAN I DID!

FIRST OF ALL, THAT'S NOT TRUE! YOU JUST DON'T KNOW HOW TO TAN!

WE WERE BOTH ON THE TOWEL THE SAME WAY, SO THERE!

LET ME EXPLAIN BEFORE YOU GET YOURSELF ALL WORKED UP...

YOU SPENT MORE TIME THAN I DID...

...LYING ON THE SAME SIDE...

PHOOEY!

CAZENOVE et WILLIAM

♪ HE LOVES ME ♪ A LITTLE ♪ LA LA LI LA LA
A LOT...

AND THEN YOU SAY I PUT TOO MUCH BUTTER ON MY TOAST... YUCK!

DING DONG

IT'S HIM!

YUCK!

SNURF SNURF

HEY, GOOD LOOKING! COME IN!

WOW! YOU'RE HOT!

MMM... YOU SMELL SO GOOD!

HERE'S A KISS FROM MY PAL, LOGAN...

SMOOCH

A LITTLE KISS FROM MY COUSIN, BULL...

YOU'RE TICKLING ME! HEE HEE!

SMACK

TWO BIG SMACKERS FROM MY BROTHER...

AND A HUGE SMA--

HEEEY... YUCK YUCK. THAT'S REALLY GROSS!

BESIDES, IF YOU LIKE IT THAT MUCH, YOU SHOULD JUST EAT IT DIRECTLY FROM THE JAR INSTEAD OF LICKING IT OFF MY SISTER.

CAZENOVE et WILLIAM

33

WHAT'RE YOU DOING WITH THE SCALE?

ARE YOU GOING TO WEIGH YOUR BRAIN?

ISN'T IT A LITTLE BIG FOR THAT?

HA. HA. DYING LAUGHING!

I'M GOING TO WATCH MY FIGURE, LIKE MOM DOES...SO I'M WEIGHING EVERYTHING I EAT.

≈PFFRRR.≈ WHATEVS!

IT'S 1 OUNCE OF CEREAL...

NO MORE.

CLING PLINK

OOPS, TOO MUCH.

THAT'S IT! I'VE ADJUSTED IT.

EEP! NOW IT'S TOO LITTLE.

HAVE TO BE PRECISE.

CLING PLINK

OOOH... TOO MUCH AGAIN.

RIGHT ON THE MONEY!

YOU CAN PUT AS MUCH MILK ON AS YOU WANT, HOWEVER, BECAUSE IT GETS ELIMINATED SUPER QUICKLY.

≈PHEW.≈ YOU'VE REALLY STUDIED YOUR SUBJECT.

FWOOSH

WHOOSH YUM... WHEN I DESHIDE TO DO SHOMESHINSH, I SHO IT COMPLETELY OR NOSH AT ALL... YUM...

GOBBLE GOBBLE YUM

AND NOW HALF AN OUNCE OF COOKIES...

CAZENOVE et WILLIAM

‡PFFF‡... I'M SO BORED...

ME, TOO, I'M BORED...

SAY, WENDY. DON'T YOU WANT TO BE BORED TOGETHER?

NO, THANK YOU! YOU'LL BUG ME AT THE SPEED OF LIGHT AGAIN AND THAT'LL GET ON MY NERVES...

FOR STARTERS, THAT'S NOT EVEN TRUE!

DON'T MAKE ME LAUGH. BUGGING'S YOUR SPECIALTY!

I'VE NEVER GIVEN YOU ANY BUGS!

BESIDES, I DON'T EVEN LIKE BUUUUGS...

PLUS, YOU ALWAYS HAVE TO BE A MEANIE!

I HATE YOU!

YES, YES. BLAH BLAH BLAH. I KNOW THE REFRAIN: I'M NOT YOUR SISTER ANYMORE, ETC., ETC.

BESIDES, I'M NOT MAKING YOU STAY. IF YOU'RE NOT HAPPY, THE DOOR'S RIGHT THERE. AND IT'S STILL MY ROOM!

OUT!

I CAN BE FINE ALL BY MYSELF AND I'M FED UP WITH YOUR DOOR AND YOUR BUGS!

SLAM

OKAY, WELL, WE ONLY USED UP FIVE MINUTES. LET'S DO ANOTHER ROUND, BUT THIS TIME WITH A FIGHT?!

COOL! HERE WE GO!

CAZENOVE et WILLIAM

35

SPAGHETTI À LA WENDY... TELL ME IF YOU LIKE IT!

MMMMM... THAT SMELLS GOOOOD!

THAT'S EXCELLENTISSIME! YOUR PASTA WITH MOZZARELLA! YOU'RE A SUPER COOKER-FELLA!

CHEF!

LOL—

HEE HEE HEE

HAH HAH HAH

HA-HA! IT'S STICKING. I'VE GOT LOTS OF IT ON MY FINGERS.

ME TOO. I'VE GOT IT ALL OVER ME!

ARE WE GOING TO BE ABLE TO EAT TO IT? HA-HA!

I HAVE SOME ON MY CHIN AND MY NOSE.

DON'T YOU FIND IT ROMANTIC, MASE?!

ON TOP OF THAT, IT'SH DELISHOUS!

SLURP

COME ON! YOU COULD EAT PROPERLY! YOU'RE OUR GUEST, LET ME REMIND YOU.

...A REAL PIG!

CAZENOVE et WILLIAM

MASON TOOK ME TO THE MOVIES...

AFTERWARDS, HE TOOK ME TO A RESTAURANT...

YUM YUM

YUM GUZZLE YUM

AND EVEN ON A CULTURAL EXCURSION...

WHOA! THIS ROCKS!

BREEEM BREEEM

NOTHING ACTUALLY ROMANTIC...AT LEAST, UNTIL...

THIS EVENING, I'LL TAKE YOU TO THE THEATER...

YOU'LL SEE. IT'S SO CRAZY!

?!

I THINK I'VE FINALLY HAD A GOOD INFLUENCE ON HIM...

LA LI LA LA LI

I LIKE YOUR DUDS, MISS!

UH... THANKS!

SO, DID YOU SEE?

THE WHOLE ROOF OF THE THEATER IS COVERED WITH PIGEON DROPPINGS...

IT ROCKS!

SERIOUSLY!

YAHOO!

ACTUALLY, I THINK MAUREEN'S INFLUENCED HIM INSTEAD.

CAZENOVE et WILLIAM

THESE NEW DRAWINGS OF DAD'S AREN'T BAD.

DID YOU SEE THIS PANTHER, MAUREEN? CHECK OUT THE TEETH.

WHAT'RE YOU CHUCKLING ABOUT? SHOW ME!

HA HA HA

LOL!

MY SISTER WITH A STINKY MR. BUN BUN.

PLUS IT'S IN HER MOUTH... YUCK!

AND THIS ONE? DID YOU SEE THIS ONE?

AH...HERE. DID YOU WET YOUR DIAPER, EH?

PHOOEY! DOESN'T SCARE ME, SO THERE!

BUT IT SHOULD...

≠GASP!≠

HURK! HURK! HURK!

ZZOOOOM

≠PHEW≠... JUST A NIGHTMARE.

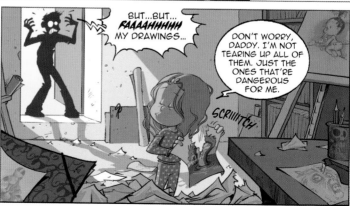

BUT...BUT... RAAAAHHHHHH MY DRAWINGS...

DON'T WORRY, DADDY. I'M NOT TEARING UP ALL OF THEM. JUST THE ONES THAT'RE DANGEROUS FOR ME.

SCRIIIITCH

CAZENOVE et WILLIAM

I'M THE ONE WHO TAUGHT MAUREEN HER FIRST WORDS WHEN SHE WAS A BABY...

OFLATO.... OFLATO...

NO, MAUREEN. IT'S NOT AN "OFLATO," IT'S A "POTATO."

OTATO! OTATO!

THAT'S ALMOST IT. POTATO.

OTATO!

OTAAATO!

AH, NO, THOSE ARE SQUASH.

AND NEXT TO THEM ARE TURNIPS.

OTATO?

SQUASS

BURNIPS

OTATO

RAPUNZ

OTATO!

OTATO!

OTATO!

COME ON YOU...

...BIG POTATO HEAD.

YES, YOU'RE A SQUISHY SQUASH.

YOU'RE THE ROTTEN TURNIP!

IF I'D ONLY KNOWN, I WOULDN'T HAVE TAUGHT HER ANYTHING AT ALL!

CAZENOVE et WILLIAM

39

SNOOORE

EVERY NIGHT, IT'S THE SAME THING...

CREEAK

MAUREEN HAS TO COME AND CAMP OUT IN MY BED...

IT KEEPS GOING ON UNTIL SHE TAKES UP THE WHOLE BED...

SNOOORE

I CAN'T STAND IT ANYMORE HERE...

...SHOULD I SCREAM OR NOT?

ZZZZZ

OH, JEEPERS!

I'VE GOT THE SOLUTION... I JUST HAVE TO STEAL MISS GLUE STICK'S BED.

I SHOULD'VE THOUGHT OF THIS SOONER...

A BED ALL TO MYSELF...

TOO COOL!

RIGHT... I HOPE THE COUCH IS FREE.

CAZENOVE et WILLIAM

40

WENDY REALLY AMAZES ME...

MOM, DAD...I DIDN'T MEAN TO DO IT BUT I MESSED UP IN MATH.

WHEN SHE DOES SOMETHING BAD, SHE PUNISHES HERSELF ALL ON HER OWN...

OKAY, I'LL GO CLEAR THE TABLE.

THAT WAY, OUR PARENTS DON'T PUNISH HER...

I'M SORRY I CAME HOME SO LATE...

...I DIDN'T SEE THE TIME.

I'LL GO WASH THE DISHES.

SCRATCH SCRATCH

IT WORKS EVERY TIME.

AS A RESULT, WHEN I'M THE ONE WHO DOES SOMETHING BAD...

I KNOW WHAT I HAVE TO DO...

UH... MOMMY ...I

I DIDN'T MEAN TO BREAK YOUR PRETTY JAPANESE PORCELAIN VASE...

I'M SUPER SORRY!

IT'S GOOD, WENDY. I APOLOGIZED.

YOU CAN CLEAR THE TABLE AND DO THE DISHES.

CAZENOVE et WILLIAM

41

A LITTLE MORE TEA IN THE CAFÉ?

BUT OF COURSE, MY DEAR MR. BUN BUN.

HEYYY, WENDY. WILL YOU HAVE A TEA PARTY WITH ME?

THERE'LL BE CHERRY PASTRY TART FOR DESSERT.

YIKES, NO THANKS!

I HAVE TO GO NOW.

COME ON... JUST FIVE MINUTES. PRINCESS RAPUNZEL IS THE HOSTESS.

YOU KNOW, MAUREEN, I'VE STOPPED DOING THESE KINDS OF THINGS NOW. I'M STEPPING INTO REAL LIFE, Y'KNOW?

THIS WASN'T REAL BEFORE?

I'M STARTING MY PROFESSIONAL WORK EXPERIENCE TODAY.

SO YOU'LL HAVE TO PICK UP YOUR LI'L CUPS AND YOUR LI'L GLASSES ALL BY YOURSELF.

TOO BAD, MR. BUN BUN. WENDY WAS GREAT AT TEA PARTIES...

AND MAKE SURE TO PICK UP ALL THE CUPS AND GLASSES...

CAZENOVE et WILLIAM

42

MAUREEN AND I RESEMBLE EACH OTHER LESS AND LESS...

MY FRIEND ROSIE'S GOING TO STOP BY TO SEE US WITH HER SON.

OH, JEEZ! LET'S GO GET READY!

ZZOOOOOMM

ZZOOOOOMM

THAT'S IT! HAIR TOUCH-UP...

MAKE-UP TOUCH UP...

PERFUME TOUCH-UP...

PISSHH

PISSHH

YOU NEVER KNOW. MAYBE ROSIE'S SON'S CUTE...

UH... MAUREEN... WHAT'RE YOU UP TO?

I'M ALMOST READY.

BOF

BOF

BOF

I NEED TO BE IN TOP FORM IF WE FIGHT WITH THIS GUY...

BOF

BOF

BOF

BOF

IN FACT, MAUREEN AND I AREN'T LIKE EACH OTHER AT ALL.

CAZENOVE et WILLIAM

43

RRRAAAAHRRR...
ENOUGH ALREADY WITH THE
DOOR SLAMMING!

THE WHOLE HOUSE
IS GOING TO COLLAPSE
IF YOU KEEP THAT UP!

ACCORDING
TO MY FATHER,
IT CAN'T FAIL.

SO WE
SHOULD SLAM
IT HARDER?

HERE
WE GO. GIVE
IT YOUR ALL.
ONE, TWO...

CAZENOVE et WILLIAM

YOU SHOULD'VE SEEN MY SISTER'S FACE WHEN WE TOLD HER SHARKS WERE UNDER THE BOAT--

WOW! LOOK AT THAT HORSE, WENDY...

IT'S AMAZING!

COME ON! LET'S GO LOOK AT IT.

I NEVER TOLD YOU, BUT I'M CRAZY ABOUT HORSES.

AH, UMM, ME TOO, TOTALLY.

THEY'RE BEAUTIFUL, OBEDIENT, FAITHFUL, AWARE...

WILL YOU LOOK AT THAT MANE, THAT SHINY BROWN. IT'S MAGICAL!

OH, YES, VERY CLASSY!

THAT GIVES IT AN AWESOME LOOK.

OH, YES. FOR SURE!

SWEET!

I COULD SPEND HOURS CONTEMPLATING THEIR MANES.

YES, YES.

ME TOO...

WENDY, Y..YOU'RE SURE YOU WANT THE SAME CUT AS THAT?

YES! YES, AND SHINY BROWN, JUST LIKE IN THIS PHOTO!

CAZENOVE et WILLIAM

HONESTLY, CAN YOU BELIEVE IT? HE'D NEVER TALKED TO ME LIKE THAT...

DEF. THAT'S TOO MUCH!

LOL. THESE PIGEONS'RE HAVING A PARTY WITH THE CROISSANTS.

YOU'RE RIGHT, EMM. THEY LOOK HUNGRY.

GREEDY GUSSES!

AND THEY'VE GOT NOTHING AGAINST A GOOD CHOCOLATE CROISSANT EITHER.

HERE, BIRDIE BIRDIE BIRDIE...

AT LEAST THEY'RE FAITHFUL!

WOW! TAKE A LOOK AT THAT!

I DIDN'T KNOW PIGEONS WERE BIRDS OF PREY?

PIGEONS...BIRDS OF PREY, YOU'RE SAYING? HMMM, I DON'T THINK SO...

BUT MY SISTER? YES, WITHOUT A DOUBT!

=SCARF= YUM! YUMMY! =GOBBLE=

CAZENOVE et WILLIAM

46

MAUREEN IS LIKE A KITTEN WHEN SHE'S TIRED...

SHE FALLS ASLEEP WHEREVER SHE IS.

SHPLOF

LOL

IT'S REALLY TRIPPY...

SNORE ZZZZ

SURPRISING...

SNORE ZZZZ...

LUDICROUS...

SNORE ZZZZ...

UNEXPECTED...

SNORE ZZZZ...

BRRRRR

PUTT PUTT

PUTT PUTT

IN SHORT, IT CRACKS ME UP. I FIND IT RATHER CUTE...

SNORE ZZZZ...

WELL, NOT ALWAYS...

SNORE ZZZZ

CAZENOVE et WILLIAM

WHEN I'M OLDER, I'LL HAVE LOTS OF BABIES...

...12, 13,14, OKAY! EVERYONE'S HERE!

WE'LL PLAY THE WHOLE DAY LONG. IT'LL BE SUPER FUN!

YOU GENTLY BRUSH THE DOLL'S HAIR, AVOIDING THE KNOTS.

FOR YUMMIES, EVERYONE'LL GET A TURN...

THERE'S ENOUGH FOR EVERYONE. DON'T PUSH AND SHOVE!

THE SAME THING WHEN THEIR DIAPERS HAVE TO BE CHANGED ONCE A MONTH...

THEY'LL TAKE CARE OF THEMSELVES.

WE'LL TAKE LONG WALKS IN THE PARK.

LET'S GO! WE'LL WALK 4 MORE MILES AND THEN GO BACK HOME!

OFF WE GO! LENGTHEN YOUR STRIDE!

AND IN THE EVENING, SHOO! EVERYONE INTO THE TOY CHEST!

YOU KNOW, MAUREEN, BABIES AREN'T LIKE STUFFED ANIMALS.

OH, YEAH? FOR STARTERS, WHAT DO YOU KNOW ABOUT IT?

CAZENOVE et WiLLiAM

WHO'S BRINGING HER LI'L SISTER A SURPRISE?

IT'S WENDEE.

LOOK AT ALL THESE MAGNIFICENT DRAWINGS I MADE ESPECIALLY FOR YOU!

CLASSY, WOULDN'T YOU SAY?!

LASSIE!

TO START, LET'S PUT ONE NEXT TO YOUR BAMBI POSTER...

BAMBI DABABDA!

AND THESE THREE HERE WILL GO SUPER NICELY NEXT TO THE WINDOW.

THESE ARE GOING TO LOOK SO GOOD IN YOUR ROOM, MAUREEN. YOU'RE SO SPOILED.

SOSPOYLD?

DON'T GO ANYWHERE. I'M GOING TO MAKE YOU SOME MORE. LOTS MORE!

AND THIS ONE... I'LL PUT IT HERE...

AND THESE TWO SUPER LOVELY ONES, INSTEAD OF THAT AWFUL JUSTIN BABY.

DON'T WORRY, I'VE GOT LOTS MORE STILL.

I KNEW I'D PAY DEARLY ONE DAY...

CAZENOVE & WILLIAM

SOMEBODY TOLD ME... ♪ ♪ YOU STILL LOVED ME... ♪

♪ SOMEBODY TOLD ME... ♪
BLECH!

SAY, MOM...
...YOU WOULDN'T KNOW WHY THERE'S FUR IN MY FACE CREAM?
DO I LOOK LIKE I'D KNOW?

I SWEAR, SAMMIE, IT'S SO DISGUSTING!
YUP! TOO WEIRD!
HAS ANYTHING LIKE THAT EVER HAPPENED TO YOU?

TOTALLY. IT'S WEIRD, I KNOW...
CRAZY.

YEAH... HMMM...MAYBE... HMMM...

ANYWAY, I THINK I'VE GOT A LI'L IDEA...

FOR GOODNESS SAKES, DON'T TELL ME THAT...

AFTER PUDGE, IT'S YOUR TURN, CUDDLES...
LITTLE CREAM LIKE YESTERDAY AND YOU'LL BE THE LOVELY COLOR OF A PEACH PIT.

CAZENOVE & WILLIAM

50

THE HARDEST PART OF MY DAILY LIFE AS A BIG SISTER...

WHAT'RE YOU UP TO, MAUREEN? ARE YOU STILL HALF ASLEEP?

YES, WHY?

IS PUTTING UP WITH MAUREEN'S SPECIAL BRAND OF LOGIC...

I SPREAD JAM ON BOTH SIDES. THAT WAY MY UPPER AND LOWER TEETH CAN HAVE THE JAM AT THE SAME TIME.

LOGIC THAT'S SOLID AS A ROCK...

WENDY, WILL YOU COME WITH ME TO LOOK FOR MY BALLOON? IT FELL ON THE OTHER SIDE OF THE ROAD...

YEAH, RIGHT. DO YOU NEED ME FOR THAT RIGHT NOW?

DEFINITELY! THAT WAY IF ONE OF US GETS CRUSHED, THE OTHER WILL BE ABLE TO BRING BACK THE BALLOON.

I'M SLEEPING ON THE FLOOR. THAT WAY MY BED WILL ALREADY BE MADE IN THE MORNING. HEE HEE.

WHATEVS!

AND WITH THIS, SHE BROKE EVERY RECORD...

WENDY, I JUST THOUGHT OF SOMETHING TOTALLY SILLY...

WELL, THAT'LL REALLY BE A CHANGE.

I THINK IT'S DUMB THAT WE'RE ALL THESE YEARS APART IN AGE...

'CUZ AFTER ALL WE DON'T LIKE THE SAME GAMES, SAME MOVIES, ALL THAT...

WE JUST HAVE TO CELEBRATE MY BIRTHDAY EVERY MONTH. THAT WAY, IT WON'T BE LONG BEFORE WE'LL BE THE SAME AGE BRILLIANT, DON'T YOU THINK?

LOOKS LIKE ANOTHER MIGRAINE'S ON ITS WAY...

CAZENOVE x WILLIAM

WOW!

JEEPERS, YOU'RE *SOO* PRETTY, WENDY.

AH, UH... WELL, THANKS, MAUREEN!

EXTRA SUPER *BEEYOOOTIFULLL!*

I LOOOVE YOUR SHINY HAIR AND ALL.

YOU'VE GOT SO MUCH CLASS.

YOU'RE HOTTER THAN ANY OTHER SISTER IN THE WORLD.

YOU'RE THE PRETTIEST IN THE WHOLE GALAXY!

WHAT? WHAT'S GOTTEN INTO YOU NOW?

YOU CAN TELL ME I'M PRETTY WHENEVER YOU WANT, TOO!

YOU'RE SO VAIN!

CAZENOVE & WILLIAM

The window in Polly's room opens with a sordid creak...

SNOORE

...Letting an icy wind enter, which little by little takes on a human shape...

It's the Terrifying Mummy Wazaro Linstone...

It draws near to its victim...It will haunt her dreams for the rest of her life...

Octopus Flesh
Shiver
THE MUMMY

MAUREEN, YOU SHOULD STOP READING THOSE SCARY BOOKS...

WHY, MOMMY? THEY'RE FOR KIDS.

YES, BUT THEY CAN STILL DISTURB YOUR SLEEP.

COME ON...I'M NOT SCARED, AND BESIDES, THESE ARE STORIES, Y'KNOW...THEY'RE FAKE.

I WASN'T TALKING ABOUT YOU...

CLICK CLACK CHATTER

...OR STOP READING THEM OUT LOUD THEN.

CAZENOVE & WILLIAM

ARE YOU READY, MAUREEN?

EXTRA SUPER READY!

≥HUFF≤ ≥HUFF≤ ≥HUFF≤ ≥HUFF≤

WOW, SHE'S GOING SUPER FAST!

HOP

HOP

HOP

YEEHAW!

OUCH!

A NEW WORLD RECORD FOR *GIVING A HUG!*

YES!

LOL! WE'RE THE BEST!

CAZENOVE & WILLIAM

AYAYAAAAA...

HONK HONK HONK SHAKA SHAKA PONK HONK! IT'S ME, KING KONG!

GRRROOOAR!

BWA-HA! MY SISTER'S HAVING A BLAST ON THE ROPES COURSE!

HA-HA!

YEEHAAAAW...

FOR SURE! A REAL MONKEY!

BUT I DON'T GET IT...WHY AREN'T YOU DOING IT?

OH, MY...

I HAVE TO SAVE ALL MY STRENGTH FOR A LITTLE LATER, Y'KNOW?

YOUR STRENGTH?

BRRRRINGGG

?!

AH, BY THE WAY, THAT'S RIGHT NOW, EXACTLY.

MAUREEEN... COME DOWN! WE HAVE TO GO NOW.

SO, MASE. NOW DO YOU SEE WHY I NEED ALL MY STRENGTH?!

LET ME GO!

LET ME GO!

RAAH.

I WANT TO STAY!

OFF WE GO. SHH. SEE YOU TOMORROW.

CAZENOVE & WILLIAM

WOW! AND YOU'RE THE ONE WHO DID ALL THAT, WENDY?!

YUP! I'VE BEEN SLOGGING AWAY!

I'M GOING TO TRAVEL WITH MY PARENTS. I'D LIKE TO EARN A LITTLE POCKET MONEY TO BRING BACK SOME SOUVENIRS.

SOUNDS GOOD!

SO I'M SELLING SOME BLACK AND WHITE DRAWINGS. THE ONES IN COLOR ARE MORE EXPENSIVE.

VERY CLASSY!

SOME NECKLACES AND BRACELETS MADE OUT OF COLORED PEBBLES...

TOO COOL!

THE HARDEST PART — IS PIERCING THEM WITHOUT BREAKING THEM.

...SOME FIGURINES OUT OF SALT DOUGH...IT TOOK ME HOURS TO SCULPT THEM.

THAT ONE THERE IS CATWOMAN...

PLUS SOME PHOTOS OF FLOWERS IN THE GARDEN.

AWESOME!

THE BLACK AND WHITE ONES ARE MORE EXPENSIVE.

⁞PFFF.⁞ AS IF. FOR THE MOMENT, IT'S BARELY EARNED ME FIVE DOLLARS.

WELL, MAYBE YOU SHOULD TRY TO SELL THEM TO SOMEONE OTHER THAN YOUR SISTER...

HMMM... YOU THINK SO?

CAZENOVE & WILLIAM

WHAT GREAT JOB COULD I HAVE WHEN I GROW UP?

MOVIE STAR...

CLASSIC, BUT IT WOULDN'T BE A GOOD FIT FOR ME.

OR LEAD SINGER IN A METAL BAND...

WOW...AWESOME CONCERTS!

OR A BUSINESSWOMAN AT THE HEAD OF A MULTINATIONAL CORPORATION. I'D LIKE THAT, TOO.

HA! MY TURN WITH YOUR PRIVATE DIARY

YEEAH!

FINALLY, I'VE FOUND MY CALLING...

HOG-TYING RODEO COWGIRL!

BUT...I DIDN'T DO ANYTHING...

CAZENOVE & WILLIAM

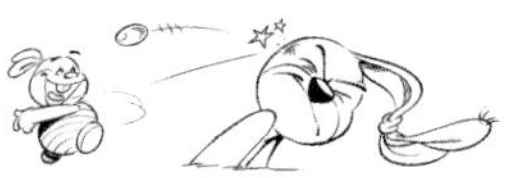

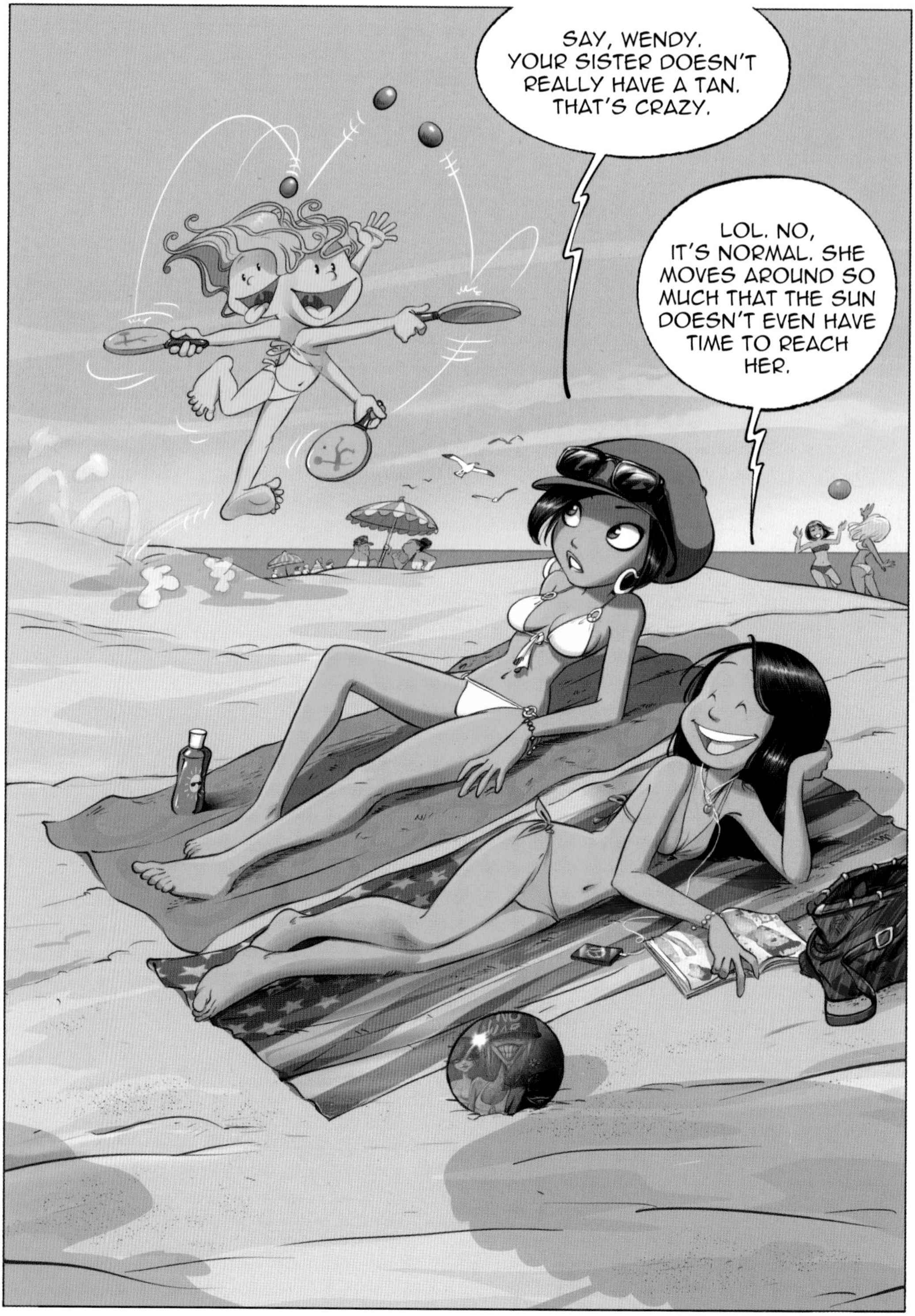
SAY, WENDY. YOUR SISTER DOESN'T REALLY HAVE A TAN. THAT'S CRAZY.
LOL. NO, IT'S NORMAL. SHE MOVES AROUND SO MUCH THAT THE SUN DOESN'T EVEN HAVE TIME TO REACH HER.

CAZENOVE & WILLIAM

EVEN WITHOUT COUNTING THE BUTTON AND THE HULK-SHAPED ROCK...

...WE STILL HAVE ENOUGH MONEY TO BUY SOME CANDY.

BUT WE WON'T GO BY THE PARK BEFOREHAND.

— OKAY?!

YOU REMEMBER IT'S THE SAME EVERY TIME...

WE PLAY LIKE CRAZY...

...WE LOSE OUR MONEY...

...AND BYE-BYE CANDY.

YOU'RE RIGHT, MAUREEN. LET'S GO RIGHT DOWN TO THE STORE.

THOSE CHOCOLATES ARE OURS!

THE STRAWBERRY CHEWS!

YUM YUM!

READY, LULU?

SUPER READY, AS USUAL!

THE TREATS ARE OURS!

BONK

RE-BONK

CAZENOVE & WILLIAM

WOW, MY NEW SMART PHONE'S AWESOME!

IT'S SWEET!

YOU GOT THE PRETTIEST ONE IN THE STORE, TOO.

I'LL TEXT SAMMIE TO TELL HER...

OH...LET ME DO IT, PRETTY PLEASE, PRETTY PLEASE!

LIKE, DO YOU KNOW HOW TO TEXT?

WHAT DO YOU THINK?

I DON'T COME FROM PLANET DUMBDUMB...

FIRST I FIDDLE WITH YOUR CONTACTS...

I FIND THE RIGHT ONE. THERE, THAT'S SAMMIE, OKAY...

AFTER THAT, I TYPE IN MY LI'L MESSAGE...

AND I EVEN HAVE THE RIGHT TO MAKE MISTAKES.

IT'S EVEN RECOMMENDED.

I GET A RUNNING START AAAAAND...

I SEND IT!

GIVE IT BACK! YOU NUTCASE!

WHAT. IT'S OKAY. I WAS JUST KIDDING, ⸗PFFF.⸗

GRAB

BWAH-HA-HA

TAKE NOTE, LULU...

THE BIGGER YOU GET, THE LESS YOU HAVE A SENSE OF HUMOR.

CAZENOVE & WILLIAM

HURRY UP, THEN, QUIIIICK...

YES, YES. JUST A MINUTE, EMMA. THIS PACKAGE IS ARMORED.

WOOOW! WHAT AN AMAZING FIGURINE.

IT'S THE WATER WING FAIRY! OH...SO PRETTY.

THE THIN WINGS, EARRINGS, JEWELRY. IT'S CRAZY! HOW'D THE GUY DO IT?

TOO AWESOME!

I LOVE THE 'SHROOM... I COULD EAT IT.

IT SEEMS LIKE SHE COULD SPEAK. CRAZY, RIGHT?

FIRST OFF, PUT HER IN A SPOT UP TOP... THESE THINGIES ARE REALLY FRAGILE.

THERRRRE...YOU'LL DO VERY WELL HERE, PRETTY FAIRY.

UMMM, AREN'T WE IN YOUR SISTER'S ROOM?!

ACTUALLY, I PUT EVERYTHING FRAGILE HERE...

IT KEEPS MAUREEN FROM BREAKING THEM WHEN SHE STEALS THEM FROM ME...

CAZENOVE & WILLIAM

YES, IF I WANT TO PUT AWAY SOME MONEY FOR VACATION I NEED TO GET MOVING...

IT SHOULDN'T BE TOO HARD TO MAKE PICTURES...AND I COULD GO SELL THEM AT THE MARKETS.

STUPID IDEA. QUICK, MY GUITAR.

HIGHWAY

OH, YEAAH!

TO HECK

RIGHT, NO MORE OF THAT.

UNNGH

THERE'S GOT TO BE SOMETHING I KNOW HOW TO DO BETTER THAN ANYONE ELSE...

HOLY COW! OF COURSE!

SMAK

I'M SO STUPID!

THUMP

DEAREST DADDY WHOM I LOVE SO VERY MUCH...

COULD YOU GIVE ME SOME MONEY, PRETTY PLEASE?

CAZENOVE & WILLIAM

STOPPP!

THAT'S ENOUGH!

YOU'RE REALLY INFURIATING, MAUREEN, YOU KNOW THAT? DO YOU WANT ME TO SHOW YOU WHAT IT'S LIKE TO HAVE A LITTLE SISTER?

UH... WELLL. I...

WHAT'RE YOU DOING, *MAUREEN?* WHAT'RE YOU DOING? WHAT'RE YOU DOING?

CAN I DO IT, TOO? TELL ME, CAN I?

PRETTY PLEASE, PRETTY PLEASE, PRETTY PLEASE, PRETTY PLEASE?

UMMMM...THIS JAM MAYONNAISE SAUSAGE GARLIC CROISSANT IS SUPER DELICIOUS.

YUM GOBBLE GOBBLE

AND I'M GOING TO READ *YOUR* PRIVATE DIARY AND GET LOTS OF GREASE ON THE PAGES. NYAH NYAH...

PEEPEE CACA

TOOT TOOT

YAHOO...

OOOH...SHE'S IN LURVE...SHE'S IN LURVE...

MASE... MASON?!

UMMM... HI, WENDY!

YOU SEE, THE DIFFERENCE IS THAT I AM NOT EMBARRASSED WHEN *I* ACT LIKE A BABY!

THE SHAME! THE SHAME! THE SHAME! THE SHAME! THE SHAME! THE SHAME!

CAZENOVE & WILLIAM

HIA-YAAAH!

I'M GOING TO SLICE OFF ALL YOUR WARTS, YOU DIRTY DEFENDER OF NICE DRAGONS!

TELL ME, HOTHEAD, DON'T YOU THINK IT'S TIME YOU ACTED LIKE A GIRL?!

ACT LIKE A GIRL?

ONE DAAAAY MY PRINCE WILL COOOOOOME... ONE DAAAY...

DING DONG

COMING!

SMACK SMACK

KISS

UH...WENDY, I THINK MAUREEN'S SPYING ON US...

AND AFTER THAT, SHE BUYS ME A VIKING WARRIOR COSTUME...

I UNDERSTAND MY SISTER LESS AND LESS...

CAZENOVE et WILLIAM

HA!

TEXAS! THAT'S WHERE I'LL LIVE WHEN I GROW UP!

TEK SASS?

THAT WORKS...

...I'VE ALREADY GOT MY STETSON.

YEEHAW!

CLASSY, DON'T YOU THINK? A REAL TEXAN.

OH, YEAH!

HEE HEE. GIVE *DALTON* A KISS FOR ME.

MY TURN TO THROW A DART TO FIND OUT WHERE I'LL LIVE WHEN I GROW UP.

ADMIRE MY STYLE.

TO INFINITY...

AND OFF WE GO THERE!

HMM...

HMM...

WHAT A SCREAM! HA HA HA! HEY, MOM...COULD YOU STITCH UP AN ASTRONAUT SUIT FOR MAUREEN?!

I ALWAYS KNEW MY SISTER HAD HER HEAD IN THE CLOUDS...LOL!

CAZENOVE & WILLIAM

65

WENDY, WENDY, HA-HA, YOU'LL NEVER GUESS...

WHY SHOULD I, SEEING THAT YOU'RE DYING TO TELL ME?

EH, WELL, AT SCHOOL EVERYONE CALLED ME THE LIONESS.

COOL, WOULDN'T YOU SAY?

THAT'S JUST LIKE ME. MY HAIR'S LIKE A MANE.

PLUS MY ASTROLOGICAL SIGN'S LEO, TOO...

THAT FITS YOU WELL, FOR SURE! I SAW A DOCUMENTARY ON TV ABOUT LIONESSES, AND THEY'RE READY TO DO ANYTHING TO DEFEND THEIR TERRITORIES, YOU KNOW...

I DEFEND MY STUFFED ANIMALS SUPER WELL, FOR A START.

AND ALSO A LIONESS IS ALWAYS ON ALERT, AFRAID OF MISSING SOMETHING...

JUST LIKE ME!

I'VE ALWAYS GOT A COPY OF THE TV GUIDE SO I DON'T MISS ANY SHOWS.

AND THE LIONESSES ARE THE ONES THAT HUNT FOR THE WHOLE FAMILY.

THEY BRING BACK FOOD.

SO THERE'S NO DOUBT, IT'S REALLY YOU. HERE!

QUEEN OF THE HUNT...

...PHOOEY! I'VE BEEN HAD!

CAZENOVE & WILLIAM

66

MAUREEN USED TO GET ON MY NERVES WITH HER BABY GAMES...

WENDYYY...WILL YOU PLAY HUNGRY HIPPO WITH ME?

PRETTY PLEASE, PRETTY PLEASE, PRETTY PLEASE?

SO I DECIDED TO TEACH HER BIG GIRL GAMES.

WHOA, WHOA, WHOA, OKAY. I'LL PLAY WITH YOU, BUT ONLY IF I GET TO CHOOSE THE BOARD GAME. I'VE GOT ONE THAT'S SOPHISTICATED.

MORE SOPHISTICATED THAN HUNGRY HIPPO?

IT'S CALLED TRIVIAL PURSUIT.

ARE THERE FIGHTS?

...BLAH BLAH BLAH QUESTIONS... BLAH BLAH BLAH PIE CHART...BLAH BLAH...COLORS...

THE LI'L PIECES ARE SO CUTE!

AND THEY DON'T SMELL LIKE PIE.

WHOEVER GETS TO THE MIDDLE WITH THEIR PIE FILLED WINS.

WANT TO TRY IT?

OH, YEAAHHH! IT SEEMS FANTASTIC...

AS I EXPECTED, SHE LOVED THE CONCEPT RIGHT AWAY.

LET'S PLAY!

LET'S PLAY!

LET'S PLAY!

LET'S PLAY!

HEEEY... OH, NO, HEY...

BUT IT WAS ESPECIALLY THE *PURSUIT* SIDE THAT SHE WAS EXCITED ABOUT.

RAAH...GIVE ME THE ANSWERS!

HA-HA! CATCH ME! CATCH ME IF YOU WANT TO FIIIIND THEM OUT.

CAZENOVE & WILLIAM

ALRIGHT, ONE LAST HAND. IT'S MY TURN TO SHUFFLE.

I HAVE A HUNCH I'M GOING TO TOTALLY WIN IT.

THERE YOU GO! I'LL DEAL. HA-HA! CATCH YOUR CARDS.

HEEEY, CALM DOWN, DORK!

IT LOOKS LIKE YOUR CARDS ARE ALL ROTTEN, WENDY...

STOP MESSING AROUND AND PLAY!

HEH HEH HEH!

ACES!

BAM!

IN YOUR FACE!

I WONNNN... I WONNNNN!

YESSSS.... I WONNNN. I'M THE BEST...

WOOHOO!

YOU SAW SHE CHEATED THE WHOLE TIME?!

AND YOU LET HER DO IT?!

YES, BUT LOOK. I CAN'T STAND WATCHING HER THROW A FIT WHEN SHE LOSES EITHER. SHE HOWLS AND JUMPS AROUND EVERY WHICH WAY. IT'S REALLY ANNOYING.

YYYEEESSSSS!

PERSONALLY, I DON'T SEE ANY DIFFERENCE.

CAZENOVE & WILLIAM

TELL ME, MY SISTER, I WANTED TO PLAY PING PONG BUT I CAN'T FIND MY ROLLER BLADES.

OH, YOU'RE HERE.

I WANTED TO LOOK IN MY ROOM AND I WOUND UP IN THE BATHROOM...

ARE YOU SURE YOU'RE OKAY, MAUREEN?

AND THIS HOUSE, HERE.

...IT ISN'T OURS. LOOK AT THE COLOR.

WHAT YEAR IS IT, ACTUALLY? HERE. BUT WHOSE WATCH IS THIS?

WENDY, YOUR SISTER'S OFF HER ROCKER. SHE'S GOT MAJOR MEMORY PROBLEMS. SHE EVEN TOOK ME FOR YOU.

OH, NO! HERE WE GO AGAIN. IT'S STARTED AGAIN.

THIS HAPPENS TO HER ABOUT ONCE A WEEK.

OH, YEAH?

YES, EVERY TIME IT'S HER TURN TO DO THE DISHES.

DISHES? WHAT A STRANGE WORD. WHAT DOES THAT MEAN?

THIS KID, I SWEAR...

MWAH HA HA HA!

CAZENOVE & WILLIAM

69

OKAY, MAUREEN. WHAT INSTRUMENT ARE YOU GOING TO PLAY TO CELEBRATE MOM'S BIRTHDAY?

TADAAAH! THE HARMONICA. *YYEEEEHAWWW!*

HAPPY BIRTHDAY TO YOU...! LISTEN.

OR ELSE THE PIANO...

THE RECORDER. IT'S GREAT, TOO!
TOORLOOOREEREETOOOO

THAT HURTS MY EARS, FOR SURE.

YOU JUST HAVE TO PLAY THE MARACAS WITH THE SALT SHAKER.

NOOOO...NOT THE SALT SHAKER...I WANT TO PLAY A REAL INSTRUMENT, TOOOOO...

OKAY, OKAY! TRY SINGING TO SEE--

HAPPY BIRTHDAY TO YOOOOUU...

WELL, WELL, WELL? IT'S GREAT, RIGHT? DID YA HEAR?

MMHMM... I HEARD.

HAPPY BIIIIRTHDAY...

CHICK KA CHICK KA CHICK

CAZENOVE & WILLIAM

70

SAY, WENDY...

UH...IS EVERYTHING... GOING WELL...FOR YOU? AND...I... YOU...WELL...

CRUNCH MUNCH

DON'T BEAT AROUND THE BUSH; ASK YOUR QUESTION DIRECTLY...IT'LL BE EASIER.

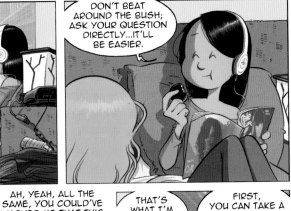

ACTUALLY... I'D LIKE YOU TO TELL ME HOW TO DEAL WITH BOYS...

D'OH!

AH, YEAH, ALL THE SAME, YOU COULD'VE WARNED ME THAT THIS WAS A REAL QUESTION.

THAT'S WHAT I'M REALLY WONDERING.

FIRST, YOU CAN TAKE A WALK IN THE PARK WITH HIM. IT'S ROMANTIC.

YOU CAN ALSO GO TO A MOVIE...AND THEN GO TO THE FAIR...IN A NUTSHELL, YOU NEED TO KNOW WHAT HE LIKES TO DO BECAUSE IT'S GOOD TO START OUT WITH THAT KIND OF THING.

OKAY! THANKS, WENDY!

AT HER AGE I WASN'T INTERESTED IN GUYS YET...

HOLY COW! MY LITTLE SISTER IS GROWING UP VERY QUICKLY!

WELL, YOU DON'T SAY. THE MOVIES, A PARK, A FAIR...

MMM...

ALL THAT SO THAT HE'LL GIVE US HIS SANDWICH... PHOOEY!

AND BESIDES, WE'RE NOT EVEN SURE IT WILL WORK.

CAZENOVE & WILLIAM

I WOULD REALLY LIKE TO HAVE THE SUPERPOWER OF *INVISIBILITY*...

...THAT WAY, I COULD FOLLOW MY SISTER EVERYWHERE.

CRAZY, *NO?!* AND THAT'LL BE OUR SECRET THEN!

JUST FOR US.

NOW YOU'RE TALKING...

YOU'LL NEVER GUESS WHAT MASON JUST TOLD ME...

HEE HEE! I KNOW IT ALREADY!

I'D SPY ON ALL HER CONVERSATIONS. I'D KNOW ALL HER LI'L TRICKS...

IT'LL STAY BETWEEN US, OKAY?!

LOL, OKAY, WENDY!

WOOW...

I COULD EVEN MEMORIZE HER PRIVATE DIARY...

THEN I'D GO TELL MY FRIENDS EVERYTHING.

HEEEYYY, GIRRRRLLLS...

WELL, WHAT'RE YOU LOOKING FOR? YOOHOO, IT'S ME.

HEEEY...DON'T GO. I'VE LOTS OF THINGS TO TELL YOUUU...

HELLLLLLP... A GHOOOOST...

MOMMMMY!

CAZENOVE R WILLIAM

72

LOOK, WENDY! LOOK HOW EXCEPTIONAL I AM AT BOUNCING THIS RUBBER BALL...

I'M UP TO 33...

WITHOUT LETTING IT FALL...34... 35...

I'M NOT SURE SHE KNOWS HOW TO COUNT PAST 40...LOL!

36... 37...

38...

SUCH A WALK IN THE PARK!

HA HA! DID YOU SEE THAT? THAT COUNTS TRIPLE...

ON THE EDGE COUNTS AS ONE AND A HALF.

SHE'S GIFTED.

YES...GIFTED AT DRIVING ME NUTS.

THAT'S FINE, YOU CLOWN. WE GET IT NOW.

SNATCH

BUT, UH--

GO BOUNCE YOUR WORTHLESS BALL SOMEWHERE ELSE!

JEALOUS!

SO...*WHAT* WERE WE TALKING ABOUT BEFORE?

YESTERDAY IN BASKETBALL, I SHOT TWO 3-POINTERS...

AND I DUNKED THE BALL AT LEAST 5 TIMES.

WOOOW..., YOU'RE SO AMAZING. MY RECORD KING!

CAZENOVE & WILLIAM

LUIGGI, MY ITALIAN PEN PAL ARRIVED AT THE HOUSE YESTERDAY.

WELCOMO TO OURA HOUSA!

HE SEEMS NICE AND WE HAVE 15 DAYS TO GET TO KNOW HIM. SO COOL!

WHAT YOU LIKEY? SPORTSI? TELEVISIONO?

YOU KNOWA BASKET BURGER?

YOU LIKEY TOMATEE?

I PUT TOGETHER A CRAZY SCHEDULE FOR US...

TUESDAY, PICNIC WITH MY BUDS...

HIKE THROUGH THE WOODS...

PHOTOS UNDER THE VIADUCT...

MONDAY, VISIT THE TOWN...

MY SISTER LET HIM USE HER ROOM...FOR ONCE SHE'D BEEN NICE.

MAKEY YOURSELFEY AT HOMEY, LUIGGI.

AND IF YOU WANT A SNUGGLY, LET ME A KNOWO.

AS A RESULT, SHE'S SLEEPING WITH ME.

IT'S TORTURE...

...YEP, IT'S THE WORST!

SERIOUSLY...

...WHEN DO YOU LEAVE AGAIN?

CAZENOVE & WILLIAM

74

WHERE IS HE? WHERE IS HE?

WE KNOW YOUR ITALIAN PEN PAL'S COME, WENDY.

HIS NAME'S LUIGGI, ISN'T IT?

POINTLESS TO DENY IT. WE WANT TO SEE HIM!

NOT WORTH GETTING EXCITED ABOUT, GIRLS...

HE'S ANYTHING BUT GLAMOROUS, OUR LUIGGI.

OHHH, AN UN-GLAMOROUS ITALIAN?

THAT EXISTS?

WELL, YOU JUST HAVE TO TAKE A LOOK...HE SPENDS HIS DAYS SPRAWLED OUT ON THE COUCH, PLAYING KIDS' GAMES.

WHAT A LOSER!

HE STUFFS HIMSELF WITH CANDY...

HE READS BOOKS FOR BABIES...

HE DOESN'T SMELL VERY GOOD.

NOTHING TO MAKE YOUR HEAD SPIN.

BUMMER!

WHOA! THIS GUY'S TOTALLY AWESOME!

...HE LOVES TV, CANDY, GAMES AND THE SAME BOOKS AS ME... PLUS HE SMELLS DELICIOUS...

ISN'T HE SO CUTE?!

YES, LUIGGI'S AWESOME!

CAZENOVE & WILLIAM

75

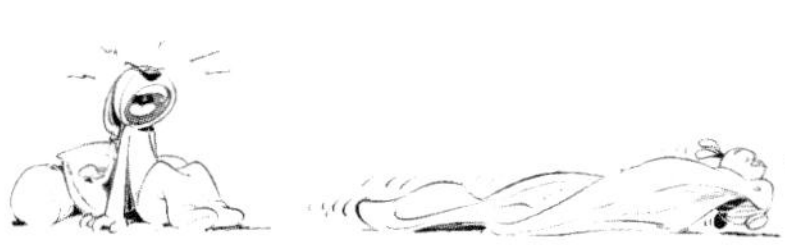

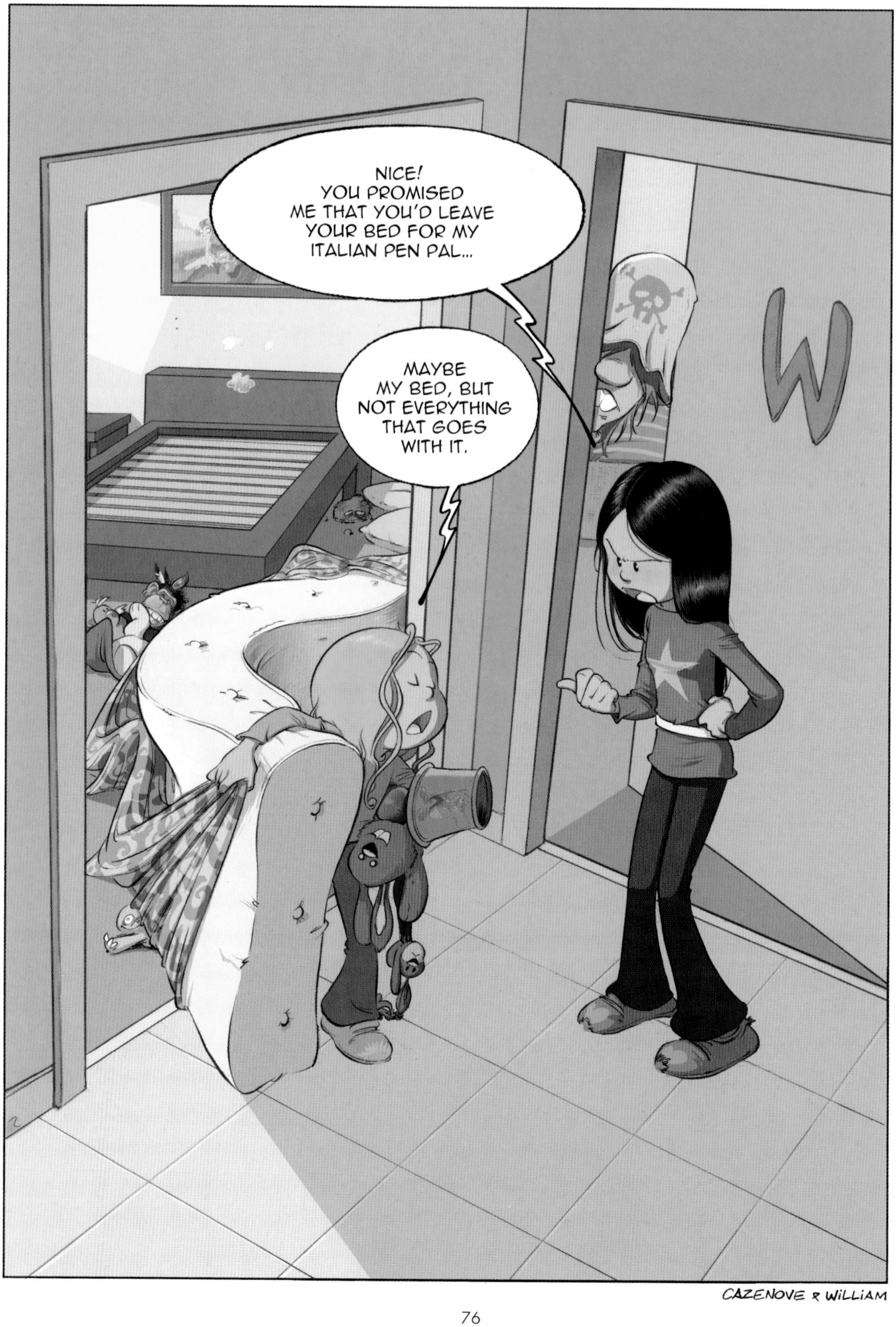
NICE! YOU PROMISED ME THAT YOU'D LEAVE YOUR BED FOR MY ITALIAN PEN PAL...
MAYBE MY BED, BUT NOT EVERYTHING THAT GOES WITH IT.
W

CAZENOVE & WILLIAM

I SWEAR TO YOU, *EMMA*, HE'S FLAT-OUT CRAZY ABOUT ME, OUR LUIGGI.

NOOOO... NO KIDDING? HEE HEE!

I SWEAR TO YOU... THIS MORNING AGAIN...

...I WAS BARELY OUT OF MY ROOM. HE FOLLOWED ME...

AND YOU CAN BE SURE HE DIDN'T LEAVE ME THE WHOLE DAY.

WHEN I WENT SHOPPING...

WHEN I WAS ON THE INTERNET...

IN SHORT, HE STUCK TO ME LIKE A ZIT ON A BOY'S NOSE.

MWA-HA-H-HA!

HEY, LUIGGI, DO YOU WANT TO COME PLAY A GAME OF CHECKERS WITH ME?

A GAMO OF CHECKERSEY WITH MIO?

YES! YOU'RE GOING TO LIKE HOW I SHOW YOU UP.

I'M THE BEST...THE BESTA, WHAT?

...PATHETIC...

NO WAY, I CAN'T BELIEVE IT. THAT LITTLE BRAT ALWAYS HAS TO NICK MY THINGS!

HE'S MY PEN PAL, OKAY?!

CAZENOVE & WILLIAM

77

YOU'RE MAKING ONE OF THOSE FACES AGAIN, WENDY...

...YOUR SISTER, STILL?!

WORSE!

LUIGGI... GETS ON MY NERVES. NOTHING INTERESTS HIM...

...THE GUY'S ALL WOBBLY!

DID YOU TRY TO TALK TO HIM?

SERIOUSLY, I DON'T STOP. BUT IT'S NO USE. IT'S OFFICIAL. I DON'T HAVE A PEN PAL ANYMORE.

UH...UM... COME STAI, LUIGGI?*

NON TI ANNOI?*

HAI VISITATO LA CITTA? HAI ACQUISITATO DEI SOUVENIR?*

SI MOLTO. COME TI CHIAMI? SAMMIE, SI?

YES YES HEE HEE

*"HOW ARE YOU, LUIGGI? AREN'T YOU BORED? HAVE YOU VISITED THE TOWN? DID YOU BUY ANY SOUVENIRS?" "YES, LOTS. YOUR NAME'S SAMMIE, RIGHT?!"

BLAH BLAH BLAH

HA HA HA

BLAH BLAH BLAH

AND SO FORTH AND SO FORTH

AND SO FORTH AND SO FORTH

HA MWAH-HA-HA-HA!

HEE HEE HEE!

IT'S OFFICIAL! I DON'T HAVE A FRIEND ANYMORE!

CAZENOVE & WILLIAM

WENDY, WHAT DO YOU CALL IT WHEN YOU DO THAT THING WITH YOUR FACE?

SMILING?

NOOOO...WHEN YOU'RE GETTING RID OF FACE THINGS?

TAKING OFF MAKE-UP?

MOISTURIZING?

BRUSHING YOUR TEETH?

EXFOLIATING?

MUD MASK?

NO, NONE OF THOSE EITHER... IT'S WHEN YOU'RE GETTING STUFF OUT OF YOUR NOSE...THEY SHOWED IT ON TV...

YOUR NOSE HAIRS?

THE THINGIE THAT YOU NEED TO GET OUT...

...IT'S ALL GROSS AND DISGUSTING...

VERY EMBARRASSING...

IT'S NOT--?

BLOWING YOUR NOSE? THAT'S IT, IT'S BLOWING YOUR NOSE!

YESSSS... THAT'S IT!

YOU'RE SO AWESOME, SISTER DEAR.

FOR ONCE, SHE UNDERSTOOD SOMETHING.

LOOK, LULU. OUR LUIGGI IS BLOWING HIS NOSE... WENDY'S THE ONE WHO TOLD ME THAT...

SHE STILL DOESN'T GET IT!

YUCK!

CAZENOVE & WILLIAM

I'M GOING. I'M GOING. STAY PUT!

HERE'S YOUR BALL.

YOU REALLY LIKE TO MAKE YOUR LIFE COMPLICATED.

DON'T GO AWAY.

I'LL BE RIGHT BACK WITH YOU.

CAZENOVE & WILLIAM

DOES THAT USE REGULAR GAS OR PREMIUM?

NEITHER OF THOSE! IT NEEDS FUEL THAT PACKS A BIGGER PUNCH: PLUTONIUM!

GROWL-IIEE

4:00

4:00

4:00

4:00

4:00

4:00

PAUSE

LOL. MY SISTER, IN TRACTOR MODE

SSNORE

YUM YUM

LA LA LA LI LA

MAUREEEEN

CAN YOU BRING ME BACK SOME TOMATO JUICE...

AND SOME CRACKERS? THANKS.

IT'S NOT FAIR! YOU ALWAYS WIN "FIRST TO GET UP MAKES THE SNACK."

TRUE THAT, YES.

YOU'VE NO CHANCE, BRAT!

I'M THE WORLD CHAMPION!

CAZENOVE & WILLIAM

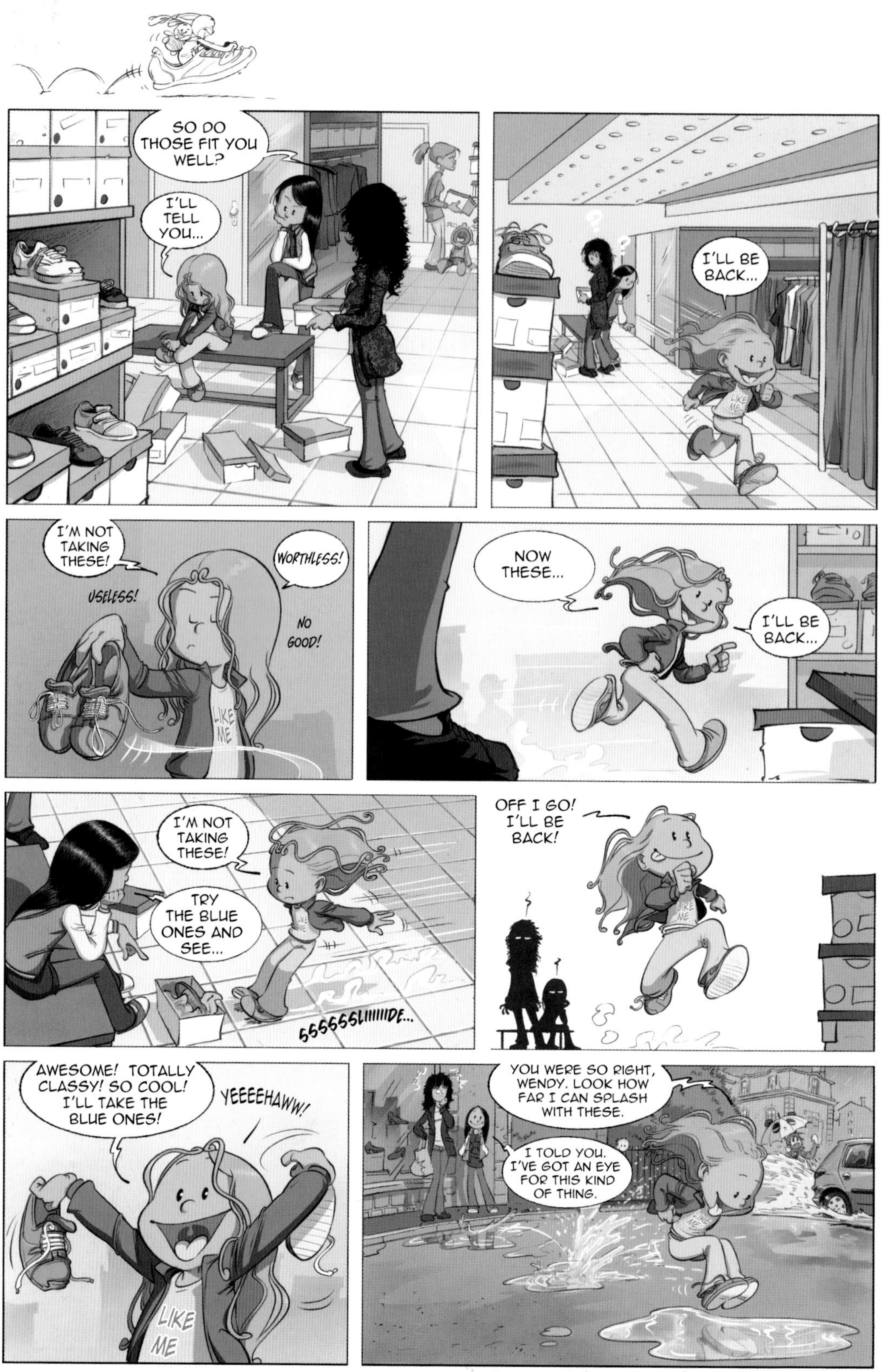
SO DO THOSE FIT YOU WELL?
I'LL TELL YOU...
I'LL BE BACK...
I'M NOT TAKING THESE!
USELESS!
WORTHLESS!
NO GOOD!
NOW THESE...
I'LL BE BACK...
I'M NOT TAKING THESE!
TRY THE BLUE ONES AND SEE...
SSSSSSLIIIIIIDE...
OFF I GO! I'LL BE BACK!
AWESOME! TOTALLY CLASSY! SO COOL! I'LL TAKE THE BLUE ONES!
YEEEEHAWW!
LIKE ME
YOU WERE SO RIGHT, WENDY. LOOK HOW FAR I CAN SPLASH WITH THESE.
I TOLD YOU. I'VE GOT AN EYE FOR THIS KIND OF THING.
CAZENOVE & WILLIAM

YOU'LL SEE, LUIGGI. THERE ARE SOME MAGNIFICENT WATERFALLS ON THE OTHER SIDE OF THE WOODS...

COME?*

THE WATERFALLS!

NO NEED TO SHOUT. HE'S NOT DEAF. HE JUST DOESN'T SPEAK OUR LANGUAGE. THAT'S ALL.

*ITALIAN FOR "WHAT?"

WAIT, I'VE GOT AN IDEA.

BONK

OUCH!

RE-BONK

YOU'RE BARKING MAD! BESIDES, WATERFALLS AND STUNT FALLS ARE UNDOUBTEDLY NOT THE SAME IN ITALIAN.

WHAT YOU'RE DOING ISN'T HELPING.

LOOK, LUIGGI... OOF! PLOINK! PLICK! PLOUP! PLOUP! SPLASH!...

WHAT YOU'RE DOING'S CERTAINLY GOING TO HELP.

RIGHT, SINCE YOU'RE GOING TO BE LIKE THAT, I'M GOING BACK HOME.

SO, KIDS... THE WALK TO THE WATERFALLS?

STUPID! LUIGGI ISN'T INTERESTED IN ANYTHING.

AND BESIDES, HE NEVER UNDERSTANDS ANYTHING, SO THERE.

CAZENOVE & WILLIAM

83

RAAAH
PFFF

PHOOEY!

TSSS...

PHOOEY!

GNN!!!

AGRRRR...

NOT HERE
EITHER.

AH, I SEE WHAT
YOU SHOWED
HER...

...YOUR NEW
TABLET...

YUP AND NOW SHE
THINKS EVERYTHING
IN THE HOUSE IS
TOUCH-SENSITIVE.

:PFFF!:
THAT DOESN'T
WORK AT ALL.
NOT HERE
EITHER.

...IT'S
DUMB...

CAZENOVE & WILLIAM

WHY THE LONG FACE, WENDY?

I'M BORED.

I WANTED TO CALL SAMMIE, BUT I ALREADY TOLD HER EVERYTHING ABOUT MY DAY.

YOU JUST NEED TO TELL HER ABOUT THE LATEST EPISODE OF "THE LOUD HOUSE"...

ALREADY DID THAT.

SO TELL HER HOW I WORE YOU OUT AT CHECKERS THIS MORNING...

HOW YOU *CHEATED*, YOU MEAN?!

OH, AND BESIDES I HAVE NO DESIRE TO TALK ABOUT THAT.

SO GIVE ME YOUR PHONE. YOU DON'T NEED IT.

HEEEYYYY! DON'T START. GIVE IT BACK TO ME RIGHT AWAY!

WOOOW... YOU'VE GOT LOTS OF TEXTS.

TAP TAP TAP

YOU'RE CRUISING FOR A BRUISING!

OKAY. OKAY. HERE. HERE. I DON'T WANT IT ANYMORE.

HEE HEE HEE!

HONESTLY, CAN YOU BELIEVE IT, SAMMIE? SHE'S OUT OF HER MIND, THE BRAT...

I ASSURE YOU, SHE GAVE ME BACK MY SMART PHONE. I'M NOT TELLING YOU HOW I SHOOK HER AROUND!

SHE'D BE LOST WITHOUT ME!

CAZENOVE & WILLIAM

HEY, MAUREEN. IS YOUR SISTER IN HER ROOM?

UM... YES. BUT WE CAN'T TALK TO HER.

EVER SINCE YESTERDAY SHE'S BEEN SAYING WE CAN'T BUG HER. SHE'S CRAMMING ITALIAN.

ITALIAN?

BUT ISN'T TODAY THE DAY THAT HER PEN PAL GOES BACK HOME?

I DON'T UNDERSTAND.

I NEVER UNDERSTAND ANYTHING WHEN WENDY DOES STUFF, ANYWAY.

HELLO, EMMA, "COME STAI?"

THAT MEANS "HOW ARE YOU?"

— UH

MAUREEN WAS TELLING ME YOU'VE BEEN WORKING AWAY AT YOUR ITALIAN?

YES! CRAMMING TO THE MAX...

WHAT'S THE POINT, SINCE LUIGGI IS GOING BACK TO HIS COUNTRY THIS EVENING?

EXACTLY! IT'S SUPER MOTIVATIONAL.

NOW I KNOW HOW TO SAY:

GO BACK HOME.

IT'S NOT WORTH CALLING ME.

NO TEXT MESSAGES.

FORGET ME!

— LOL.

CAZENOVE R WILLIAM

WELL, THAT'S IT, FINALLY. ⸮OOF!ⸯ

LUIGGI'S GONE BACK TO HIS COUNTRY! *YAAAAHOOOOOO!* PARTY TONIGHT!

LOL. YOU'RE EXAGGERATING. YOUR PEN PAL WASN'T A MONSTER.

NAH. BUT YOU KNOW... HE'S SO ODD. HE DIDN'T UTTER THREE SENTENCES IN TWO WEEKS.

YES, YOU'RE RIGHT.

WELL, IT WENT OKAY FOR ME. I SPOKE WITH HIM A LITTLE BIT.

YOU HAD A CHANCE TO IMPROVE YOUR ITALIAN TOO. IT'S A PITY.

PLUS YOU WOULD HAVE HAD A REASON TO GO THERE ONE DAY!

IMPOSSIBLE, SAMMIE! LEARNING TWO LANGUAGES AT THE SAME TIME...

...IS TOTALLY BEYOND ME.

TWO LANGUAGES? HOW'S THAT?

HEYYY, WENDY...

...DID YOU SEE? I SCULPTURATED A PUFFYCHAIR WITH LEAVES FROM THE SYCAMORICUS TREE. IT'S PRETTYJONES, DON'T YOU THINK?!

MAUREEN DIALECT. IT'S REALLY HARD IN ITSELF ALREADY.

CAZENOVE & WILLIAM

WOOOW...YOUR DOLL HOUSE IS TOO CUTE...

CAN I PLAY WITH YOU?

SORRY, MAUREEN, BUT WE'RE NOT PLAYING NOW, YOU KNOW...

AND NO...

...WE'VE GOT ARCHITECTURE HOMEWORK ABOUT DUE TOMORROW.

ARCHIE TEXTURE?

...CARPENTRY... LOAD-BEARING WALLS...

CARP ENTRY?

IT'S FAR FROM BEING A CINCH. VERY DIFFICULT STUFF.

HERE, THERE ARE 2½ INCHES. THAT MAKES IT 6½ FEET FOR REAL.

YEAH. YOU HAVE TO WORK TO SCALE. IT'S EXTRA TOUGH.

ATTIC BEAMS...

WITHOUT FORGETTING THE ENTRANCES.

SHOOT!... THIS IS GOING TO TAKE US AGES...

YOU SEE, MR. BUN BUN, MY SISTER EVEN MANAGES TO SPOIL THE NICEST GAMES.

OKAY! SHE'S GONE. I KNOW HER. SHE WOULD'VE ATTACKED OUR HOUSE WITH HER DINOSAURS.

IN THE MIDDLE OF THE WATER WING FAIRY'S BATH, ON TOP OF IT...

...COME ON, RAPUNZEL, GO TO BEDDY-BYE.

CAZENOVE & WILLIAM

A POINT FOR ME!

NO, I DON'T THINK SO...

TUNK

IT'S MY POINT...IT'S A NEW RULE...SHE WHO MISSES THE TABLE HAS WON.

WHERE'D YOU SEE THAT ONE?

LIKE, HELLO?! ANYBODY HOME?

NET! IT'S MY POINT.

IT'S A NEW RULE.

TONK

ANOTHER POINT... MISSED SERVICE, THAT'S MINE, TOO.

TUNK

GRUMPH!

TONK

OW!

TUNK

YOU ALSO GET A POINT IF YOU HIT YOUR OPPONENT.

ARGH...

YOU REALLY WANNA GO THERE, BRAT?

UHM...

12, 13, 14...

NOT BAD, EH?!

TUNK

TUNK

TUNK

TUNK

OW, OW, OW. THAT'S AGAINST THE RULES.

CAZENOVE & WILLIAM

THE GUESTS HAVE FINALLY ARRIVED.

YES! IT'S UP TO US TO PREPARE THE APPETIZERS.

TUT-TUT. DON'T TOUCH THE KNIFE, MISS CATASTROPHE.

I'LL CUT THE SAUSAGE. YOU TAKE CARE OF THE CHIPS.

NYAH NYAH NYAH. PHOOEY, I REALLY CAN DO IT ⸮PFFF.⸮

LOOK, WENDY. I PUT THE OLIVES IN COLORED BOWLS. IT'S PRETTIER, DON'T YOU THINK?

AND SINCE WE DIDN'T HAVE ENOUGH TOOTHPICKS, I ALSO USED MATCHES.

LOL!

HOW MANY THINGIES OF CHEESE AND THINGAMAJIGS OF TOMATOES SHOULD I SPREAD?

EMPTY THE JARS. IF NOT, THEY'LL GO BAD.

VOOEEEEEEEEEEE

FINK

00:00

HMMM...THE LITTLE SAUSAGES OVER HERE, ALL WARMED UP...

THE BACON CHOUFFLES ARE SHO DELISH. THERE ARE EVEN REGULAR ONES.

SHO WHAT'SH THE FLAVOR OF THE REGULAR ONES?

CRUNCH

YUM

MWAHAHA

OOH, THEY'RE SO CUTE!

YUM

AAAH

HHMMM

LET US THROUGH, PARDON US, PARDON US...

HOT PLATES COMING THROUGH.

IF YOU WANT SOME YOU JUST HAVE TO MAKE YOUR OWN!

CAZENOVE & WILLIAM

REMIND ME ABOUT SOMETHING. YOU'RE HOW OLD, MAUREEN?

WHY? ARE YOU LOOKING FOR A PRESENT FOR MY B'DAY?!

DEFINITELY NOT. BUT IT'S BAD, REALLY BAD, TO SUCK YOUR THUMB, Y'KNOW?

OOOPS!

WELL, IF YOU WANT TO STAY A BABY YOUR WHOLE LIFE...

IT'S NOT MY PROBLEM.

BUT YOU CAN BE SURE THAT IF YOU KEEP IT UP, WE'LL BE ABLE TO PUT RINGS ON ALL YOUR TEETH!

IMAGINE IT?!

IF SHE DIDN'T UNDERSTAND IT WITH THAT...

SUCK SUCK

SUCK SUCK SUCK

I'LL TAKE THE EMERALD AND THEN THE BLUE DIAMOND.

SUCK

THA WORKSH FOR BRACELETS OR ISH IT FOR FINGS?

RINGS, I THINK.

SHE DIDN'T UNDERSTAND A THING!

CAZENOVE & WILLIAM

91

PASS ME THE JAMALADE, PRETTY PLEASE.

THE WHAT?

YOU CAN'T SAY "THE MARMALADE" LIKE EVERYONE ELSE?

I SAID WHAT I WANT, SO THERE!

YOOOHOOOOO... A MEGA SPLASHERY IN THE SWIMFINLING POOL!

≠PFFF.≠

I LOVE BOOKSWIMMING ON A BUNCH OF PILLOWNONESS.

WHATEVS.

INSECTS

MAUREEN, YOU HAVE TO STOP...

...WITH INVENTING WORDS EVERY 3 SECONDS.

YOU'RE SAYING THAT 'CUZ YOU'RE A LOSERIO AT INVENTAGING WORDS!

INSECTS

BESIDES SOUNDING LIKE A MORON, YOU WON'T KNOW HOW TO SPEAK CORRECTLY ANY MORE WHEN YOU'RE BIG.

I'LL TALK ANY WAY I WANT.

INSECTS

SO, MISS MAUREEN...HMMM... YOU HAVE EXPERIENCE AS A...SODATOR...

...A CERTIFICATE IN NABERETTE...

AND TRAINING IN RANGEAGE OF BOOKINESS...IS THAT RIGHT?

UH...

CAZENOVE ℛ WILLIAM

WATCH OUT FOR PAPERCUTZ™

Welcome to the fabulous fourth THE SISTERS graphic novel, featuring those feisty female furies, Wendy and Maureen, by Christophe Cazenove and William Maury, from Papercutz—those bookswimming naberettes dedicated to publishing great graphic novels for all ages. I'm Jim Salicrup, the Editor-in-Chief and official Maureen translator, and I'm here to take you behind-the-scenes at Papercutz and tell you more about our most exciting new project...

As we said in THE SISTERS #3, Papercutz is launching not just one all-new graphic novel series, not just two all-new graphic novel series, but an entire new line of graphic novels created just for you! That is if you're interested in graphic novels featuring great characters in amazing situations having awesome adventures with a touch of romance. If so, Charmz is just what you've been looking for! Charmz, the all-new imprint from Papercutz. We already told you about CHLOE, STITCHED, and SWEETIES, so now let's take a look at two more Charmz titles...

Rocketing to the bookseller or library near you is ANA AND THE COSMIC RACE, by Amy Chu, writer, and Kata Kane, artist. Just imagine all the fun of a show like *The Great Race*, but having the contestants travel through time and space! Well, that's exactly what happens when megaquadrillionaire (Maureen's not the only one making up words!) and genius inventor Dr. Laslo issues a challenge to the students of the Galactic Scholastic Federation. It's an interstellar scavenger hunt, better known as the great Cosmic Race. These students are the ones selected to compete: "Airy" Weathers, from the Crab Nebula; BbooBhoo of Alpha Centauri; Wiggly Carter, Jupiter Federation; Keio Maeda, New Tokyo City; Ekene Botha, South African Federation; Inge Olsen, United European Nations; Ana Silva, North America; and Lonnie Gupta, Mumbai Junior School of Technology. Super-student Ana Silva is determined to win but the stakes heat up when she interacts with the brooding Keio and charming Ekene—and she really likes them. With everything on the line, will Ana let her complicated feelings get in the way of her dream? And will Keio or Ekene win The Cosmic Race or Ana's heart?

...And then there's Maud or Mademoiselle De Laroche, if you prefer, although she seems to prefer to be called THE SCARLET ROSE. After the horrendous murder of her father, she discovers she has a grandfather, a noble count living in Paris, where she must now live. There she has an embarrassing encounter with The Fox, a masked Robin Hood-like rogue, who robs from the rich and gives to the poor. Maud is immediately smitten by this mysterious hero of the people. While her stern grandfather struggles to tame Maud's wild spirit and introduce her to proper Society, she rebels by secretly becoming a Fox-like masked marauder—The Scarlet Rose. This graphic novel series, filled with adventure and romance, is written and drawn by Patricia Lyfoung.

To give you an even better idea of what to expect from ANA AND THE COSMIC RACE check out the preview on the following pages. For more information and sneak previews of Charmz titles, and all the latest Papercutz news, be sure to visit us at papercutz.com. And don't forget to contact us and let us know what you think of everything we're up to! We suspect you won't want to miss the rangeage of bookiness that will be THE SISTERS #5 – coming soon to booksellers and libraries everywhere!

Thanks,

Jim

STAY IN TOUCH!

EMAIL: salicrup@papercutz.com
WEB: www.papercutz.com
TWITTER: @papercutzgn
INSTAGRAM: @papercutzgn
FACEBOOK: PAPERCUTZGRAPHICNOVELS
REGULAR MAIL: Papercutz, 160 Broadway, Suite 700, East Wing, New York, NY 10038

Special Preview of Ana and the COSMIC RACE

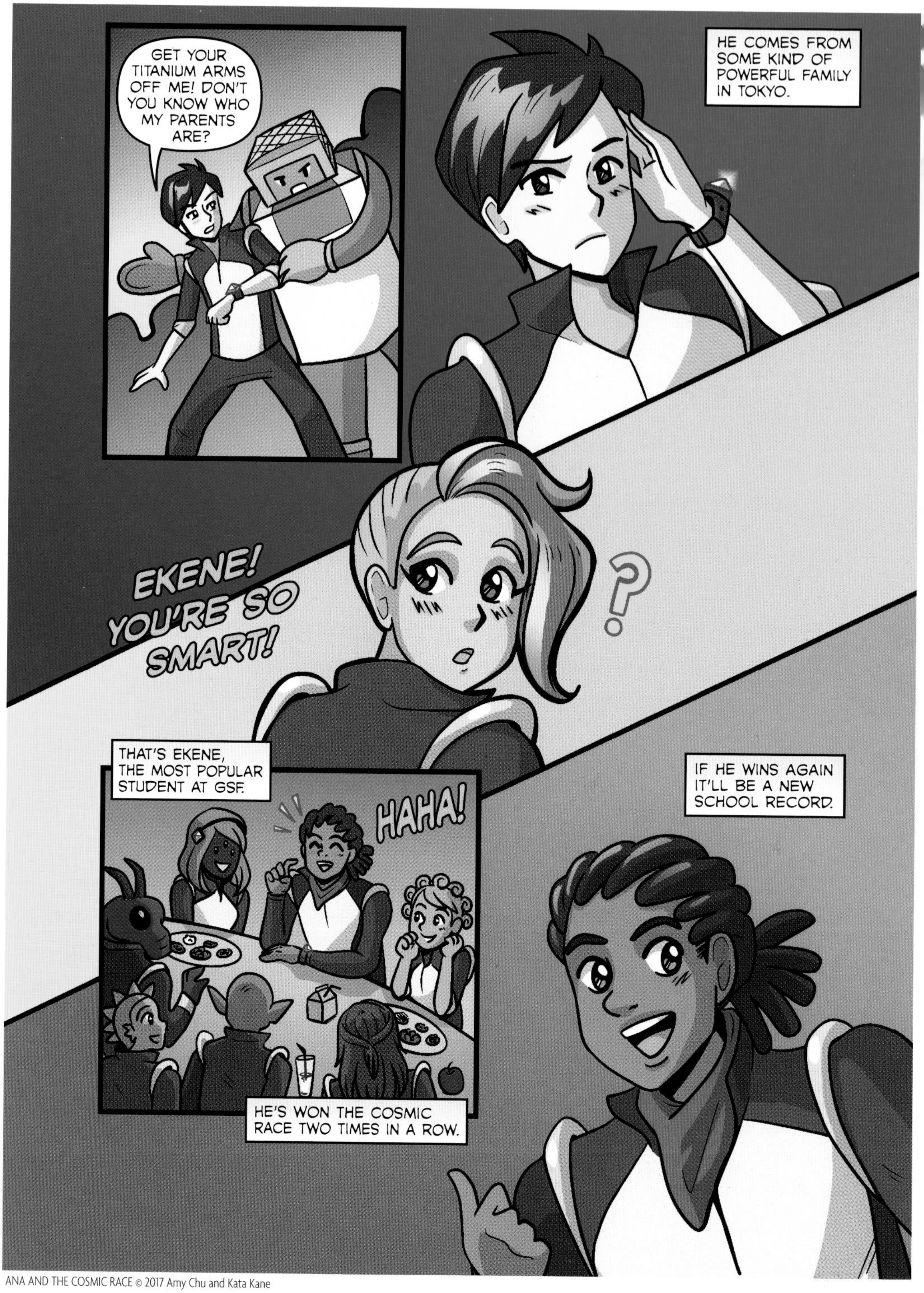
GET YOUR TITANIUM ARMS OFF ME! DON'T YOU KNOW WHO MY PARENTS ARE?
HE COMES FROM SOME KIND OF POWERFUL FAMILY IN TOKYO.
EKENE! YOU'RE SO SMART!
?
THAT'S EKENE, THE MOST POPULAR STUDENT AT GSF.
HAHA!
HE'S WON THE COSMIC RACE TWO TIMES IN A ROW.
IF HE WINS AGAIN IT'LL BE A NEW SCHOOL RECORD.

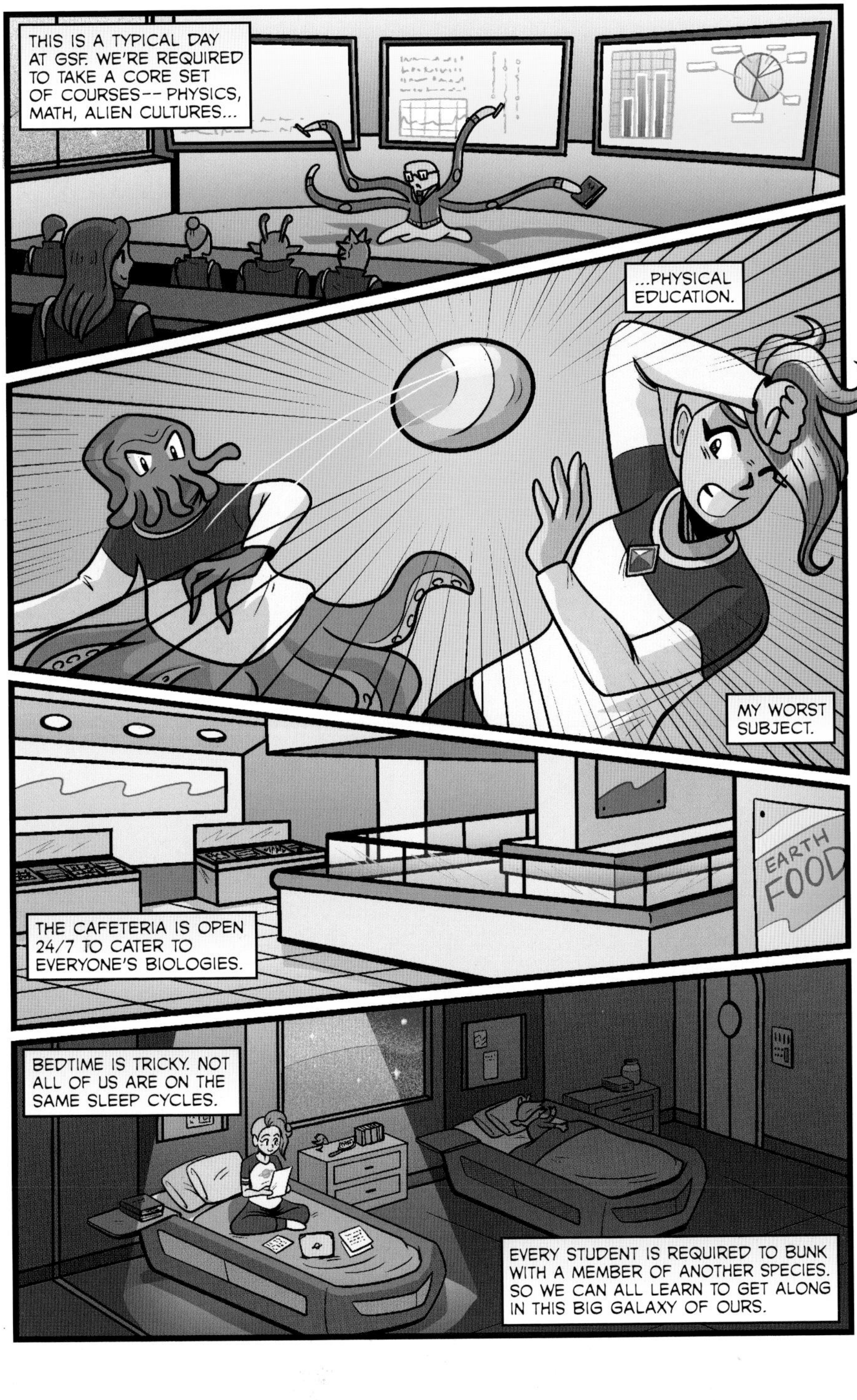
THIS IS A TYPICAL DAY AT GSF. WE'RE REQUIRED TO TAKE A CORE SET OF COURSES-- PHYSICS, MATH, ALIEN CULTURES...
...PHYSICAL EDUCATION.
MY WORST SUBJECT.
EARTH FOOD
THE CAFETERIA IS OPEN 24/7 TO CATER TO EVERYONE'S BIOLOGIES.
BEDTIME IS TRICKY. NOT ALL OF US ARE ON THE SAME SLEEP CYCLES.
EVERY STUDENT IS REQUIRED TO BUNK WITH A MEMBER OF ANOTHER SPECIES. SO WE CAN ALL LEARN TO GET ALONG IN THIS BIG GALAXY OF OURS.

ANA AND THE COSMIC RACE is Available Now at Booksellers Everywhere!